I0760296

CLASH BY NIGHT

BOOKS BY DAVID KEENER

Clash by Night
Finders Keepers *
Road Trip
An Unlikely Hero
The Whispering Voice

THE THOUSAND KINGDOMS SERIES

Bitter Days *
Death Comes to Town *
The Rooftop Game

ANTHOLOGIES AS EDITOR

Fantastic Defenders
Fantastic Detectives *
The Forever Inn *

* *forthcoming*

CLASH BY NIGHT

David Keener

T

Tannhauser Press

This is a work of fiction. All characters and events portrayed in this book are fictional, and any resemblance to real people or incidents is purely coincidental.

Clash by Night

v1.0hc

Published by Tannhauser Press
www.tannhauserpress.com
Fredericksburg, VA 22407

ISBN: 978-1-945994-78-4

Packaging by Worlds Enough LLC
www.worldsenough.com
Cover by Luca Oleastri
Copyediting by Donna Royston

For Ronald Balfour and Walter Huchthausen, two of the Monuments Men from World War II, who gave their lives in the service of protecting priceless works of art for future generations.

CONTENTS

ESCAPE

EXTRAS

CLASH BY NIGHT

Mission Personnel

Monumentalists

Emily Dunkirk: Team Lead for the group of art experts and art historians accompanying the mission. USA.
Steve Kushner: Overall Mission Commander for the recovery effort, contracted by the Monumentalists. USA.
Ester Tomkin: Kushner's assistant, a Monumentalist. Pacific Union.
Rich Miller: Foreman for the artist contingent. Hand-picked by Emily Dunkirk. Multi-lingual. United Kingdom.
Anton Ahoub: Captain of the *Khufu*, the riverboat taking the mission up the Amazon River and into the war zone. Egyptian.

+ 5 other curators and art historians

Ghost Team

Fang Li: Ghost One. Commander. Ex-Special Forces. Chinese.
Travis McCloud: Ghost Two. Experienced mercenary from a famous family of mercenaries. Republic of Texas.
Laney Sanders: Ghost Three. Experienced mercenary. USA.
Ophelia Foxx: Electronic Warfare Specialist (EWS). Nigerian.
Armel Harrison: Driver for the Armored Personnel Carrier (APC), *Paladin*. Pacific Union.

AMAZON RIVER BASIN, 2114

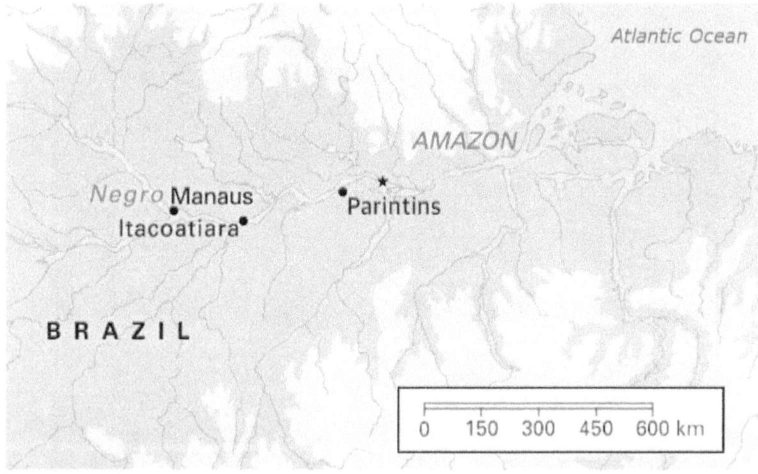

The Amazon river basin in Brazil, with the position of the Monumentalists' One World United Retrieval Mission marked by a star.

DAY 1

The Dancers, by Edgar Degas, 1900. Pastel and charcoal on paper. OWU Catalog #226.

This drawing was included in the One World United Art (OWU) Exhibition, a traveling art exhibition sent around the world to promote peace, understanding, and collaboration. The entire exhibition disappeared in 2082, in Brazil, at the outset of civil war.

01. Planning

Behind Coalition Lines, 14:54
Amazon River, 565 km east of Manaus

Emily Dunkirk pushed open the door of Kushner's cabin and a waft of cool air hit her in the face, a welcome relief from the oppressive tropical humidity outside. She was the last to arrive at the meeting, thanks to the deliberately late notice from Ester Tomkin, Kushner's assistant. The other team members had already dragged the room's wicker furniture into a rough circle. A holo projector resting on a rough-hewn wooden coffee table in the center displayed a slowly rotating, three-dimensional satellite view of the city of Manaus, looking somewhat the worse for wear thanks to regular bombing by the Chinese.

Heads turned to acknowledge Emily as she entered. Ignoring Ester's ill-concealed smirk, she took a seat next to Captain Ahoub, a tall, fit Egyptian in his late thirties. He was the commander of *Khufu*, the fifty-meter-long riverboat they were traveling on.

Steven Kushner was standing in what Emily, after past experience with the mission commander, assumed was a carefully practiced pose. With his designer outdoor gear and trademark salt and pepper hair without a single strand out of a place, he looked like a high-powered CEO on a safari. She looked over at Tomkin and noticed that she was holding a microcam focused on him.

Emily shook her head.

Unbelievable. Was it too much to ask for a leader who was focused on the job and not public relations?

What they were doing was dangerous. No matter what risks they mitigated with their planning, they were going into a war zone.

Fang Li, the leader of Ghost Team, sat on a couch, impassive as always, delicately holding a cup of tea in his scarred hands. Ghost Team was the five-person mercenary team hired to assist with the mission. They had a history of working with the Monumentalists, including one previous recovery mission with Kushner. Ophelia Foxx, Ghost Team's Electronics Warfare Specialist (EWS), sat next to Fang; she was in charge of anything electronic, from comms to the drone swarm that provided surveillance and security for their activities.

With a pointed glance at Emily, Kushner said, "Now that we're all here, I can tell you that the mission is go." He nodded gravely, facing directly at Ester's hand-held camera. "We're going in. It's up to us to rescue the One World United Art Exhibition, which went missing here in Brazil during its worldwide tour thirty-two years ago. More than two hundred priceless works of art, thought lost forever, but now they've surfaced." He paused, lifting his chin minutely to look more resolute. "We *will* rescue these works of art. We will not let these precious artifacts of our global culture disappear again. We are the Monumentalists."

Despite herself, Emily felt goosebumps on her arms. Kushner might be an insufferable idiot, but he really was an excellent orator.

Even if he wasn't really a *believer*.

An immense amount of artwork had gone missing during the Time of Troubles that had descended on the world in the latter part of the twenty-first century. Global warming had generated a toxic mix of war, famine, man-made plagues, terrorism and population migrations. The situation had been ripe for looting on a scale not seen since World War II, when the Germans, Russians and many others looted every museum and art collection they could. Their organization, the Monumentalist Foundation, was dedicated to recovering lost and stolen artwork. It was a spiritual successor to the Monuments Men, formed during WWII to find, preserve, and return artwork stolen during that smaller-scale conflict.

Emily had gotten involved with the Monumentalists in college, helping to recondition recovered paintings that hadn't been stored properly by their looters. An art historian and soon-to-be museum curator after this mission, she believed wholeheartedly in the organization's mandate. Kushner, on the other hand, seemed far more interested in glory, not to mention the completion bonus for a successful recovery. She wouldn't be surprised if he had a ghostwritten memoir, or maybe a biographical documentary, in the works.

The mission commander paused long enough so that his opening statement could easily be edited into a dynamic soundbite. "Ophelia will provide a detailed briefing." He gestured in her direction, then stooped to pour himself a cup of tea.

Ophelia stood up, a slim Nigerian with close-cropped hair and non-military gold hoops dangling from her ears. "This is Manaus," she said. "More than 1400 klicks up the Amazon River from the coast. Located at the mouth of the Rio Negro, where it feeds into the Amazon. Currently one of the strongpoints still held by the Batistas, though not for long if the Chinese have anything to say about it." Emily knew that resource-hungry China had made stabilizing Brazil a priority and were backing the faction that, largely thanks to their extensive help, appeared to be winning the decades-long civil war.

Ophelia grinned. "The Batistas are losing. Badly." The city projection darkened into a nighttime view. As details faded, a tracery of glowing lines appeared and outlined the buildings. Explosions rippled across the city. "Near nightly bombing by the Chinese, mostly focused on the downtown area, military targets and infrastructure."

Fang said, "We figure they're going to make a big push in about ten days, once they've softened up the opposition enough."

"How sure are you?" Emily asked.

Fang gave her a considering glance. "They could move sooner, maybe in five days, if they're willing to risk a phased roll-out. But they're typically more conservative than that."

Emily nodded. Fang had formerly been Chinese Army Special Ops, so they'd have to trust his insights into Chinese military activities. She still wondered how he'd ended up as a mercenary.

"Folks," Kushner said gravely, "this gives us a ten-day window to get in, get the paintings and get out before the big push starts."

"Five days," Emily corrected. "We need to be conservative, here." Kushner shot her an irritated glance. He hated being upstaged.

"Right," Ophelia responded. "Over here on the southeast side of the city, the *favela*." The map zoomed in on that area, then several windows appeared around the edge showing photos of watery channels lined by rickety-looking shacks, sometimes even stacked on top of each other. "Think of it as a poverty-stricken Venice, made of wood and scraps. Our target is a low-rent warehouse complex on the edge of the *favela*." The image obligingly focused in on the complex. "Six warehouses, surrounded by razorwire. South side has a dock extending into a private lagoon that's set off by more fencing that extends underwater. Looks like eight to ten guards at any given time.

"The word from the Fuzzy Pandas is the paintings were delivered this morning, to the warehouse closest to the dock." At that, smiles broke out around the room. Knowing that the cache was heading toward Manaus, they'd already made arrangements to infiltrate the city by boat. Not the *Khufu*, but a smaller, nondescript local vessel. "Our hackers confirm that this is just temporary, before they get transshipped to the buyer, so the paintings won't be here for long."

Emily leaned back. "Do we know who the buyer is?" She ignored Kushner's glare.

"Negative," Ophelia said. "We know the seller, a General Marcos Diego, but security on negotiations has been too tight to ID the buyer. We only know *where*, because the Fuzzy Pandas cracked the subsidiary comms." She spread out her hands and smiled radiantly. "Batista online security rots."

Kushner walked over and stood next to Ophelia. "Before we discuss taking the complex," Kushner said, "I think we'll need more refreshment." He gestured at the teapot sitting next to the holo projector. "Emily, go get us some more tea, please."

She raised her eyebrows. "Seriously? Isn't that what you have an assistant for?"

Kushner struck a command pose, then said in his mellifluous voice, "Now, Miss Dunkirk."

While Tomkin tried to hide her triumphant smile, and the others looked away in, perhaps, sympathetic embarrassment for her predicament, Emily stood up, fuming. She grabbed the tray the teapot was on and left the room.

She returned a short time later with a new tray, sweating from her foray into the stiflingly hot outdoors. By then, they were discussing the extraction, i.e. - what had to happen in order to get away with the loot. She poured out a cup of tea, and added two lumps of sugar, just the way Kushner liked it.

Kushner said, "The getaway boat drops the cargo container with the paintings in the water here." He pointed to a spot downriver from Manaus. Emily took advantage of the pause and handed him his teacup. He nodded with mock graciousness and took a sip. "Then Ghost Team's APC hooks up to the container and travels underwater to rendezvous with the *Khufu*."

Emily had seen images of the cargo container, which was almost half as long as the trailer of an eighteen-wheeler truck. It would be on the boat they'd be using to infiltrate the city. She had no doubt that the APC could get to Manaus underwater, although how quickly was a good question. But dragging the cargo container back downriver some seventy klicks seemed problematic to her.

"Do we have an alternate egress?" she asked, sitting down next to Captain Ahoub.

Fang said, "Upriver, fifty klicks and then overland to Colombia. We have a route mapped out." OK, so one alternate egress. And if the enemy twigged to their underwater capability, then both alternatives were compromised.

Kushner frowned at her. "We've taken all the variables into account."

Emily tried not to goggle at him. Anybody who thought they'd identified "all the variables" in a lightning heist of two billion credits of priceless artwork from behind enemy lines right before a big military push was, well, an idiot.

The mission leader continued on as if she hadn't deigned to interrupt him. "We'll make at least one more stop this afternoon, then time things so we pass Bang Hai in the morning." Emily saw Captain Ahoub straighten up and pay closer attention as Kushner covered details that affected his riverboat.

Ostensibly, *Khufu* was carrying a humanitarian mission chartered by the United Nations—the doctors and medical staff made up the bulk of the boat's passengers. "Bang Hai" was the nickname the Western media had applied to the Chinese forward military base (located near what had once been the thriving metropolis of Parintins) after reporters had revealed the base's extensive use of Brazilians as "comfort women" for the troops.

Kushner straightened up. "We can do this, folks. We have the expertise, we have the plan and we will bring the world's cultural heritage home." He held a resolute pose for a moment, playing to Ester's camera.

As the meeting broke up, Ahoub flashed her a wide grin and patted her hand, before he left. Tomkin sauntered out without collecting the tea service, having apparently decided that Kushner had made it her responsibility.

"Emily," Kushner said, "stay after for a minute."

Once the cabin door closed behind Fang and Ophelia, the mission leader cleared his throat. "I expect loyalty from my troops, not insubordinate and uninformed questions."

Emily straightened up and considered him for a long moment. How big a fight did she want to have with him? Was it worth it? Would it change anything?

She gritted her teeth and said, "Understood."

He nodded and gifted her with a smile that didn't reach his eyes. "I'm glad you see it my way." He patted her on the shoulder and watched as she collected the cups, saucers and teapots on a tray.

Outside, still seething, she heaved the tray into the river.

02. Playing Catch-Up

Behind Coalition Lines, 16:15
Amazon River, 552 km east of Manaus

Emily caught up with Captain Anton Ahoub in his usual place. Whenever he wasn't on the bridge or in his cabin, he was always at the bow. The *Khufu* was a working riverboat, not a tourist craft, and she had to pick her way over ropes and around machinery to get to where he stood leaning over the railing.

Without looking at her, he said, "Kushner doesn't like you."

She snorted. "You think?"

He turned toward her. "If I may ask, Em, how did you end up working for him?"

"Think of me as the gift he didn't want. He wasn't given a choice." She leaned on the railing next to him. At his raised eyebrows, she added, "He's done four recoveries for the Monumentalists. The first three were successful, I mean, like really successful. Textbook precision operations. People thought he walked on water."

"And the fourth?"

"The Clementine Recovery, named after a billionaire art collector who hid his collection during the Time of Troubles. And then died without revealing its hiding place." She shook her head. "Mostly junk, he didn't have much in the way of taste. But twenty-six of the paintings, oh my. World-class. Totally.

"After the Fuzzy Pandas dived on the collection's location, Kushner spent a week planning the perfect heist. By the time they went in, somebody else, probably the Russians, had found out about it, too. Kushner's team got in first, actually got their hands on the core paintings. But as soon as the competition showed up, he made just about every wrong decision he could. Even Ghost Team couldn't salvage the situation for him. The only saving grace was they extracted without any major casualties, mostly 'cause Ghost Team is savage dangerous."

"So Kushner's not flexible?"

"No," Emily responded. "He plans like a banshee, really, really works hard at it. But as far as I can tell, they're 'green-light' plans. They only work if everything goes right." She grimaced. "If he didn't miss any variables."

"That's not good," Ahoub said. "Brazil, well, she demands flexibility." He patted her hand. "And you?"

She chuckled mirthlessly. "You could drop me in a pond, and I'd start organizing things."

"I believe you," Ahoub said in a bemused tone. "He certainly didn't like all your questions, though."

"Well, the faction of the Monumentalists that doesn't think he walks on water," Emily said, "they jammed me on his team to help with the planning and execution. But he's basically freezing me out. Which is why I need you to fill me on what I missed during my tea run."

Behind Coalition Lines, 20:04
Amazon River, 520 km east of Manaus

Kushner reclined on the couch in his cabin and moved his hands in intricate patterns. The details of his planning were scattered across his virtual sensorium, obscuring his view of the room around him. Based on the latest satellite updates Ophelia had provided to him, he was fine-tuning the route and timing for their nighttime approach to the warehouse complex where the paintings were waiting for transshipment. Floating in with the tide—the Amazon was a tidal river, even this far inland—and gone well before dawn.

The way he figured it, success was all in the planning. With a carefully crafted plan, all you needed was competent grunts to carry it out. That was really the essence of military planning. They'd be in and out like ghosts, with nobody the wiser. Long gone before anybody even knew anything had happened.

Finesse.

This was how you planned a mission.

Tighter even than his plan for the Clementine recovery. He felt a surge of anger. It hadn't been his fault the Clementine thing had gone wrong. Circumstances beyond his, or anybody's, control. Even the best generals lost a battle every now and again. At least he'd gotten everybody out safely.

But this mission, this was going to go smooth. By the numbers.

He started as someone knocked on the door, then he swept the plan details aside. "Come in."

Ester stepped into the room and closed the door behind her. Approaching, she said, "Our little Emily is going to be a problem, isn't she?"

Kushner grinned sourly. "Undoubtedly."

"I have some ideas on how to deal with her." She tilted her head. "Maybe sideline her somehow, let Miller run her part of the mission."

DAY 2

Wheat Field With Cypresses, by Vincent Van Gogh, 1889. Oil on canvas. OWU Catalog #41.

A majestic horizontal composition, which Van Gogh regarded as one of his best summer landscapes. He painted it while he was staying in a mental asylum in Saint Remy, when he was allowed to make short walks and paint outside the asylum.

The canvas shows a golden wheat field under whirling clouds with blue mountains in the background. On the right, two darker cypresses draw the attention, with two smaller cypresses on the left. One can almost feel the wind roiling the clouds and the wheat field.

03. Bypass

Behind Coalition Lines, 10:11
Amazon River, 496 km east of Manaus

Emily gazed through the bridge window at the river, marveling at how many guises the river could take on. The morning sun slanted down, exposing a riot of colors from the vegetation that lined the shore. *Khufu* cut through a light, shallow mist, generated by the cooler water meeting the warming air. She caught a glimpse, then, of just how the mighty river could entrance and ensnare men like Ahoub, draw them in and make them content to make their living on the vast and ever-changing waterway.

It was like a painting that changed every day, sometimes even multiple times in a single day.

Emily turned toward Ahoub and found him watching her closely.

He smiled. "She's a fascinating river, isn't she?"

"Yes, I've never seen anything like it." Right now the river was beautiful like a dream, but only an hour previously they'd been passing dead towns, bombed out ruins where countless people had lost their lives, all swiftly disappearing under the encroaching jungle.

Ahoub pointed at the wide, curved display panel in front of him, which showed about a dozen video feeds from drones and observation points on the riverboat. "Alas, here comes trouble." In one of the views, Ester Tomkin was laboriously climbing the narrow stairs up to the bridge.

Emily groaned. Trust Kushner's assistant to ruin a perfectly good morning.

The door slammed open. "There you are," Ester said accusingly, as if Emily had been hiding from her.

"Indeed," Emily said drily, "here I am."

"Steven has a task for you," she said, somewhat breathlessly after the exertion of climbing the stairs in the tropical heat. She was still trying to score points against her, Emily decided. Ester was the only person who ever called Kushner by his first name. "We're going to be passing the Chinese base soon and they'll be watching us. Steven wants you and a couple other women on deck as a distraction." She held out a flat white box perhaps fifteen centimeters long and half that in width.

Glumly, Emily took the box. As Ahoub looked on with curiosity, she opened the box, revealing a pink, polka dot bikini inside. A very skimpy bikini that she would never have purchased for herself. The type that the Brazilians she'd met on the coast had referred to as *fio dental*, or dental floss.

She glowered at Ester who was trying reasonably hard to look like she wasn't pleased with herself for humiliating Emily again. Then she looked sidelong at Ahoub, who was smiling because, well, he was male. Enough said. She punched Ahoub in the upper arm with one knuckle extended, which had to have hurt just a bit but only made Ahoub smile more widely.

War Zone (Coalition-Dominated), 11:22
Amazon River, 483 km east of Manaus

Emily Dunkirk hated sunbathing with a passion.

She was a doer, somebody who accomplished things, not a debutante who lounged around like some sunscreen-covered model with a sediment tan looking to be ogled. She was the type of person who went to the beach and actually went swimming. She hated even more that she'd been ordered to lie out on the forward deck of the *Khufu*, along with the three prettiest females of the ship's medical staff.

In Kushner's estimation, despite their United Nations credentials and their cover as a humanitarian medical relief effort, a bit of a distraction couldn't hurt as they traveled up the Amazon River past Bang Hai.

A deep rumble in the sky distracted her. Shading her eyes with her hand, she looked up and saw a sleek-looking jet fly overhead, then turn upriver. Her implant helpfully superimposed "Chengdu J-46 Fighter Bomber" on her vision, thanks to a geo/military data upgrade provided for the mission by Ghost Team. At successive intervals of about a minute, seven more fighter-bombers followed. Probably heading to Manaus to drop more bombs on the rubble. Hopefully the bombing wouldn't destroy the warehouse that was the target of *Khufu's* secret mission.

As the bombers rumbled into the distance, the riverboat cruised slowly by the extensive base that occupied the southern bank of the river.

After another thirty minutes, she'd had all she could take.

"I'm done." Emily stood and slipped into her sandals.

The other women, two nurses and a young doctor from Global Doctors, looked up at her and giggled. The doctor, Gwyn Chambers, a long-limbed blond from Australia, said, "You've got to learn to relax, Em."

"I'll relax later." By which she meant, after the mission was done. All they'd just done was pass the first hurdle.

Of course, the others didn't know about the mission. They weren't stupid. They knew something clandestine was going on, but they really were here for the relief effort. As long as they could administer aid to people in need, they honestly didn't care about world politics or hidden purposes. It heartened her sometimes to think that people like her scantily-clad companions, as well as the other members of the relief effort, existed. People willing to go to extreme lengths for low or non-existent pay just to help other people that they'd never met.

As far as she'd been able to discern, the prevailing opinion on board was that the hidden objective of the relief effort was American-spawned espionage. This, despite the fact that no single nationality dominated the mission participants that had padded the relief effort's roster. Nobody had gotten a whiff that it was all an elaborate cover for a heist.

She picked up her towel, wound it around herself and walked back to her quarters. While she quickly changed into cargo shorts and a sleeveless flowery top, a message popped up in her sensorium from Miller, her foreman among the mission's art contingent.

> Ester just sounded me out re: could I handle the art stuff if you're not available
>
> They're planning something
>
> Watch your back

She smiled grimly, then left her cabin and made her way down to the aft hold. She put her hand on a scan plate next to the door. There was a hum and a green glow as her hand was scanned, then the door clicked as the lock released. She pulled the door partly open, then slipped into the compartment beyond, a cavernous space that ran approximately a third of the length of the riverboat

Ceiling-mounted white lights shown down on *Paladin*, a sleek, high-tech military Armored Personnel Carrier belonging to Ghost Team. The front of it looked like a tank, complete with a dangerous-looking main gun. The back was elongated, with room to transport a small military unit.

Emily stopped in her tracks and started laughing.

Instead of its usual drab, military coloring, the APC was bright pink with white polka dots. Just like the bikini Emily had been wearing only a short time before. The APC had highly advanced digital camouflage capabilities; somebody had clearly programmed it to emulate her bikini.

Travis McCloud popped out of the hatch on top of the APC, grinning from ear to ear. He was a large, broad-shouldered military vet from the Republic of Texas, with long, shoulder-length, sandy hair. "Howdy, darling. Loved the outfit."

She stopped next to *Paladin* and peered up at him. The lights above turned his hair into a halo around his head, which was easily the closest he'd ever come to being an angel. "Don't count on ever seeing it again."

He laughed and disappeared back into the vehicle as she began clambering up the ladder. A moment later she descended from the hatch into the APC's dim interior. Most of the light came from the bank of screens in front of Ophelia Foxx, Ghost Team's EWS, some of which were showing exterior scenes of the *Khufu* and others showing freeze-frame shots of Emily in her bikini.

"I'm going to kill Kushner," Emily said, glancing pointedly at the screens. "You're not ever going to let me forget this, are you?"

"Nope," Travis said, chuckling. He was sitting in the co-pilot seat, leaning back strategically in a way that emphasized his sculpted chest and impressive musculature. He'd been pursuing her in a steady, good-natured way for most of their journey. She knew for a fact that he'd already bedded at least two of her fellow swimsuit models. Since the other mercenaries weren't around, she assumed they were probably racked out in their bunks.

"When this is over," Ophelia added, "you're goin' viral, girl. I'm going to put these on the net."

Emily shook her head sadly, playing along. "Just what I always wanted to be...a museum curator and a notorious net model. Yay."

Travis pursed his lips. "And your parents never thought you'd amount to anything."

Emily gestured at one of the screens; it was showing a picture of her as she stood up, but the other three women were also visible. "Are men really that easily distracted?"

Ophelia and Travis looked at each other, then, almost in unison, nodded and said, "Yes."

Emily sighed and rubbed her forehead. "We're doomed," she said, pretending to ignore them as they laughed at her. "On the other hand, what are the Chinese up to?"

Ophelia said, "Well, they've got three flybabies following us, just to make sure we don't do anything nefarious too close to their base. They're too busy with other stuff to watch us for long, though."

"Um, flybabies?"

Ophelia gave her a look like she hadn't done her homework. "Little, disposable, solar-powered, micro-drones about a half-centimeter in diameter that float on a tiny air jet." She flashed a grin full of perfect white teeth. "I figure they'll drop the detailed monitoring by tomorrow. I'll surreptitiously deploy some of our own eyeball drones in about an hour...I didn't dare have them out anywhere near the base. Right now, all we've got up is the crappy UN swarm they're expecting us to have."

"Plus," Travis said, "nobody's going to be stupid enough to attack us within close view of the Chinese."

Emily nodded. She was sure the Chinese coalition would simply love the public relations windfall of rescuing a United Nations humanitarian mission, but suspected it would be considerably more difficult to find someone stupid enough to attack them this close to their core assets.

"What about egress? I thought that part of the plan looked weak." They both stared at her with blank expressions. "Look," she said, mildly exasperated, "I'm not going to go running back to Kushner."

Ophelia and Travis exchanged a look, then Travis said, "Best is obviously a quick in-and-out with nobody the wiser. Otherwise, all scenarios are dealing with a limited set of options. You can get the cargo container out by boat, get it out by dragging it behind the APC underwater, or hide it somewhere submerged for later retrieval. That's pretty much it. The biggest problem with a contested pursuit is disengaging from enemy forces for long enough to make any of those options viable."

Ophelia added, "Kushner may be satisfied with his two alternatives, but if the shit hits the fan, the situation is going to be much more fluid than that."

"Yeah, that's what I thought."

Travis grinned at her. "Hey, you're smarter than I look."

04 . Unplanned Deviation

War Zone (Coalition-Dominated), 15:36
Itacoatiara, 270 km east of Manaus

Emily leaned on the railing next to Doctor Gwyn Chambers as the riverboat eased slowly toward Itacoatiara's decrepit excuse for a dock, their third stop of the day since passing Bang Hai. Their impending arrival had already been noticed, as well as the giant red cross emblazoned on the sides of their vessel that announced its humanitarian mission. Children thronged toward the dock, waving and yelling. Drums sounded a staccato rhythm.

According to her implant, Itacoatiara had once been the third largest city in the state of Amazonas, with a population of some one hundred thousand. That must have been a long time ago, because most of the town had long since been reclaimed by jungle. All that remained was a ramshackle village that looked like it had been built out of the loose wooden debris of the old one. Towering trees were growing where paved streets had been and colorful orchids covered mounds that had probably once been buildings. It looked like one of Monet's impressionistic paintings, but overlaid with a tinge of despair that the master painter had never tried to capture.

"The drums announce that we're welcome visitors," Gwyn said, brushing a blond lock away from her face. "Otherwise, they'd go into hiding." She glanced over at Emily. "Especially with all those children. They're much prized by some of the war bands running rampant in Amazonia."

"Amazonia?"

"This whole region," Captain Ahoub said from behind them. He took a position at the railing next to Emily. "Amazonas and the surrounding states of the Amazon river basin. They've always been culturally distinct from the rest of Brazil. More so, now, after so many years of war."

Emily smiled at him. "How do you stand it?"

Ahoub quirked his lips. "It's a beautiful land, at least when nobody's shooting at you. And I try to spend most of my time well away from the front lines." He rubbed unconsciously at his neatly trimmed goatee. "The trick is to know when the front lines change."

Gwyn asked, "And you can tell this?"

He shrugged. "So far." He pushed away from the railing with a smile and walked away to direct some of his crewmen.

Gwyn craned her head to look at Ahoub as he walked away, then looked back at Emily. "You go, girl," she said.

Emily colored. "I'm not—"

"You should be," she said, chuckling at Emily's embarrassment. "Dr. Gwyn has spoken."

Emily shook her head in bemusement. It wasn't worth arguing about. She hadn't come on this mission for romance. And she didn't need the distraction, either.

As for the riverboat captain, Emily suspected that Ahoub's success had a lot more to do with his relentless attention to detail than any sort of sixth sense regarding possible danger. She wondered why he'd accepted the mission; he didn't seem like the type of person to deliberately venture into an imminent war zone.

On the plus side, *Khufu* had gotten a few strategic upgrades out of the deal, including upgraded comms to facilitate interfacing with Ghost Team and an obsolete, but still useful, UN-caliber drone swarm. Not even close to what Ghost Team had, but better than most of the other low-margin river runners. Ahoub's ship had already possessed a salvaged Tempest P-12 Defense System (another helpful identification compliments of her implant's military data upload from Ghost Team), so *Khufu* was reasonably well armed.

On the negative side, anywhere between here and Manaus could become the front lines at any time. And any untoward revelations regarding *Khufu's* secret mission could jeopardize their UN-mandated protection as a humanitarian mission.

At least Ahoub was cautious, as she knew well from working with him on the security arrangements for these humanitarian stops. Ahoub had the Tempest gun unit deployed from its internal storage compartment as a visible deterrent whenever they made landfall. Emily was all in favor of visible deterrents. She figured the best way to avoid trouble was to make sure it never started.

In addition, Ahoub had four crewmembers on guard duty carrying Mannlicher smart guns, a popular automatic weapon from South Africa. Travis McCloud and Laney Sanders, two of the three combat operatives from Ghost Team, provided security for the medical tents they'd be setting up on shore. Only the most dire cases, typically those involving serious surgery, would be brought on board.

"Hey, take a look," Gwyn whispered, interrupting Emily's reverie. "Is your Kushner guy actually going ashore?"

She craned her head and spotted Kushner and Ester about five meters away, where the gangway would be deployed once they'd come to a stop.

"I guess so," she said. "Probably wants to get some footage of himself fraternizing with the little people."

They watched as the boat drifted to a halt. Ropes were exchanged with natives on the dock, and tied off. Within a few minutes, *Khufu* was securely docked and the crew was sliding the gangway into place. Kushner marched down the gangway, flanked by the Ghost Team mercs and followed by two more of *Khufu's* security people. Ester filmed the procession from the deck.

Emily said, "Sometimes I hate it when I'm right."

War Zone (Coalition-Dominated), 16:22
Itacoatiara, 270 km east of Manaus

Laney Sanders, call sign Ghost Three, stood outside the main medical tent and cursed the weather under her breath. A rainstorm had swept through, dropping rain on her for about thirty minutes and leaving her totally drenched. The only upside seemed to be that the rain had temporarily driven the mosquitoes into hiding. This is what she got for losing the damn coin toss with Trav, Ghost Two, who'd gotten the cushy duty of being on guard within the tent.

He'd also sent her several taunting messages, in his own inimitable Texas style. Her favorite, during the height of the rainfall:

> OH, NO, I can't take the
> DRUMMING on the roof.

The natives didn't seem to be bothered by the weather. They'd patiently stood in line, the lure of real medical attention obviously outweighing any desire for shelter. At least it had been a warm rain.

From the corner of her eye, she spotted Kushner stepping out of one of the rickety buildings, where he'd taken shelter. He was followed a moment later by his lackey, Ester. Laney raised her eyebrows as it became apparent that Ester was filming him. She couldn't recall any secret missions she'd ever been involved with in which the principal felt a need to record his activities. She watched askance as Ester passed him, then, walking backward, recorded a three-quarters view of the mission commander striding confidently through the village.

Finished with her shot, Ester approached Laney. "Kushner wants to get a shot with you next."

Laney fixed her with an icy stare. "No."

Ester's eyes widened in surprise. "What?"

"I said no." She pivoted slightly to face the woman directly, moving her rifle to parade rest and deliberately drawing Ester's attention to the weapon. "Working mercenaries don't want publicity." Behind Ester, Kushner suddenly clutched his right side, then keeled over.

Laney keyed her comm. "Kushner's down, looks medical, but we need a security check and a doctor."

Ester looked around wildly, then screamed when she spotted Kushner lying in a crumpled heap.

"*On it,*" Ophelia said. "*No enemy activity in your area. No heat sources but the line of natives.*"

Ester screamed, "Help him!"

Laney strode over to the mission commander, looked down at his contorted posture. Over comms: "He's still breathing, but he's definitely unconscious."

Doctor Gwyn Chambers burst out of the tent with Travis right behind her, carrying a medical bag.

05 . Command & Control

War Zone (Coalition-Dominated), 18:15
Itacoatiara, 270 km east of Manaus

Fang leaned back in the APC's padded chair and looked on impassively as Ghost Team discussed what they were calling either the "Command Crisis" or the "Emily Situation," depending on who was speaking.

"Look," Armel said, "she can't be worse than Kushner." He was Ghost Team's APC driver, and also, at twenty-nine, the youngest person on the team. The rest of them inescapably looked like military veterans, but he simply came across like a thin, black, middle-class teenager, someone who should be playing online twitch games with his friends, not piloting a multi-million-cred piece of military gear.

Laney said, "I like her, but she's a rank amateur. She's going to get somebody killed."

Ophelia rolled her eyes. "You just think she's *muy caliente.*"

"Well, she is," Laney and Trav said at the same time.

Laney added, "Doesn't mean I want to work for her."

"Situation goes south," Trav drawled, exaggerating his Texan accent for effect, "like if Kushner can't do it, is she going to stand and deliver? Or head for the hills?"

"Stand, I think," Fang said. "She's got some backbone."

"Kushner's gone soft." Ophelia put pictures of Kushner and Emily side by side on the main screen. "He's thinking retirement, not mission. Whatever Emily Dunkirk is, she's stubborn. Is she trainable?"

Ghost Team wasn't a democracy, but whenever possible Fang liked to get everybody's input. They were all stakeholders in the outfit, after all. Laying his own interpretation on top of the discussion, Armel was positive about Emily. Ophelia was ambivalent about Emily as mission commander, but had more serious issues with Kushner. Trav and Laney were clearly concerned about her reliability under pressure. As for himself, he thought that Kushner had Emily beat on planning, but Emily had a better grasp of the dynamic nature of an operation.

"I don't see any justification for executing the escape clause," Fang said. "We've had worse clients. Anybody remember Kurdistan?" Everyone but Armel grimaced. That had been before he'd joined their team. Kurdistan had been a nightmare. "Let's just do this by the numbers and get out as fast as we can."

War Zone (Coalition-Dominated), 19:09
Itacoatiara, 270 km east of Manaus

"Well, he's alive," Gwyn said, rubbing her forehead and looking tiredly at Emily, Ester and Fang. "We managed to get him stabilized."

"What happened to him?" Emily asked.

"Best I can tell, he picked up a variant of Kielson-Bauer, one of the war viruses from a couple of decades ago. There's pockets of wicked stuff like that throughout Brazil." Gwyn shrugged. "They never got adequate spread on the countermeasures and they haven't had the infrastructure to isolate and eradicate that type of threat in years."

Ester asked, "Is he...is he going to be all right?"

"I can't make guarantees," Gwyn said. "He's not exactly the healthiest specimen of a man his age that I've seen, you know. But we've got quality medical capabilities on board, so, yes, I think he'll pull through. It's going to take a while, though."

Fang asked, "How long until he's recovered?"

Annoyed, Gwyn snapped, "Look, the secret mission you guys got going on that I'm not supposed to know about...yeah, he's not going on it."

"All right," Emily said, relieved that Kushner was going to be all right. As much as she disliked him, she didn't want him to die. She wasn't exactly heartbroken that he'd be sidelined, though. She turned to Fang. "As second in command, I am formally assuming control of the mission." Gwyn looked at her in surprise, apparently unaware of her place in the command structure. Probably not a surprise given how Kushner treated her.

Fang said, "I concur."

"You can't," Ester sputtered. "You're not qual—"

Fang swiveled and fixed Ester with a glare that silenced her. "The mission command structure exists for a reason. As of right now, Ghost Team answers to Miss Dunkirk."

Emily glanced at Fang, caught his eyes. "The mission is still go, then." She looked back at Gwyn. "You didn't hear any of this. And you won't speak about it to anybody else."

Gwyn nodded.

War Zone (Coalition-Dominated), 20:17
Itacoatiara, 270 km east of Manaus

Emily closed the door of the *Khufu's* main room behind her. The coolness was a stark contrast to the muggy heat outside. Miller, a rangy, balding art historian that she'd drafted as the foreman for her team, looked up at her from a couch. A few off-duty crewmen were gathered in a corner watching something on a flexxi.

"Any news?" he asked.

"Yes," she said. "Gather up the *artistes*. Someplace private." She smiled at the term "artistes," which had been bestowed in playful jest upon her team by Ghost Team's own Travis McCloud. Naturally, her folks had seized upon the term with gleeful abandon. It was apt; they were all art historians, museum curators or otherwise associated with the fine arts community.

A few minutes later, Miller had managed to herd all six of her artistes, seven counting herself, into the medical staging room, now unused since the *Khufu* had already ceased medical activities for the day.

Standing in front of them, Emily felt a pang of guilt as her crew looked at her expectantly. “Folks, the mission is definitely still on.” There was a smattering of half-hearted applause. “And without Kushner.” The applause got noticeably louder, with a few muted cheers mixed in. Kushner was not particularly well-liked. “As of just a little while ago, I officially took over as mission commander.”

More applause, as well as a few spirited catcalls.

“About damn time,” Miller said. “Kushner couldn’t find his arse with—”

“Maybe Ghost Team should be in charge,” Sanford interrupted. He was an art historian, tall and gangly and sporting what Emily considered to be a pretentious goatee. “You don’t have any tactical experience.”

“Oh, shut up,” somebody called out. “You’re just quoting Tomkin.”

Another person added, “Everybody knows you’re sleeping with her.”

Well, she hadn’t known, but now that she did, it felt nice seeing Sanford turn red and shut up. She’d picked him for her team because he was a hard worker, and supremely knowledgeable about art, which generally made up for his incessant complaints. Seeing him quieted by embarrassment was almost like a guilty pleasure.

"Oh, Captain, my Captain," Miller said, eliciting a few chuckles and defusing the situation in his own laconic fashion. "I, for one, think that our odds of success have just gone up."

"Thanks," Emily said. "And thank you to all of you, too, for volunteering. All I can say is, we are not pulling a Clementine, no matter what happens."

She saw nods from most of her team members. They were all here because they believed in the goals of the Monumentalists. As for Sanford, she simply ignored his glare.

DAY 3

Madame Theodore Gobillard (Yves Morisot, 1838-1893), by Edgar Degas, 1869. Oil on canvas. OWU Catalog #74.

Edgar Degas was a French Impressionist painter best known for his pastel drawings and oil paintings. After meeting Yves Morisot, he approached her sister, Berthe Morisot, a fellow Impressionist painter, with a request to paint Yves' portrait.

While the painting is unfinished, it nevertheless elegantly showcases the subject, from the contour of her face to the flow of the ruffles of her dress.

06. Unexpected Hurdle

War Zone (Coalition-Dominated), 16:03
Amazon River, 166 km east of Manaus

Emily stood at the bow near Ahoub's favored viewing position, her face shadowed by a straw hat one of the Itacoatiara natives had given her, and watched the sights as the *Khufu* chugged slowly up the Amazon River. She was mesmerized by local wildlife. There were birds everywhere: ducks, various types of parrots, larks, lapwings, black hawks, cranes, and so many more that she didn't recognize. She found herself wishing she'd brought a field guide for birds with her.

For her, though, the highlight was the pink-skinned dolphin that paralleled their course for a while, leaping out of the water again and again as it played in the ship's bow wave. The fresh-water dolphins had been almost extinct before the Time of Troubles; without interference, their numbers had bounced back.

Except for the occasional Chinese jet passing far overhead, the scene she was observing probably wasn't much changed from 1913, when Theodore Roosevelt, the twenty-sixth president of the now much diminished

United States, traveled through Brazil collecting specimens for the American Museum of Natural History. She'd reread the former president's account of his travels weeks ago, when the possibility of a mission to Brazil had first been raised.

Of course, the reason it wasn't much changed was heartbreaking. Decades of war and the inexorable encroachment of the ever-present jungle had erased so much. Towns, cities, power lines, roads, farms, and the bones of millions of people, all gone beneath a verdant blanket of green. Between the Time of Troubles and their own civil war, the estimates were that Brazil had lost more than ninety percent of its population.

She'd never thought she'd ever visit Brazil, and especially not the wild, untamed Brazil that Roosevelt had described. After all, the country had been engulfed in civil war for longer than she'd even been alive. She'd also never thought that she'd ever be leading an art recovery mission for the Monumentalists. Funny how a chance meeting in college, getting involved in art restoration for the organization, had eventually led to this journey up the world's mightiest river.

She hoped she was up to the challenge.

After leaving Itacoatiara in the morning, the *Khufu* had spent the day working its way slowly but steadily upriver, making stops whenever Captain Ahoub detected visible evidence of inhabitation, which was, surprisingly, not difficult. Though it did require the ship's observation swarm, given that the river was more than ten kilometers wide in places. In most cases, the natives lined the shore, waving and shouting, and beckoning them in, which was a fairly large clue.

Emily figured it was a testament to two things. Communities still extant at this point in Brazil's interminable civil war most likely had their own lookouts and spotted them approaching. It wasn't as if a big white ship with a giant red cross on either side was inconspicuous.

And, as became increasingly evident when talking with patients, despite shocking losses in available tech, there was still a mixed low-tech/high-tech grapevine ensuring that most everyone already knew of the humanitarian mission making its way up the Amazon. As a result, even outlying villages had had time to arrange for their sick and lame to get to a friendly village or, in some cases, just a random section of the shore from which they could flag down the riverboat.

Ghost Team's more capable drone swarm helped in assessing the security aspects of each approach, making sure they weren't pulling into an ambush. While Captain Ahoub's crew provided visibly armed security on deck for each visit, Ghost Team took precautions, as well. Fang had made it clear to her and Ahoub that at least one member of Ghost Team must be in their combat suit at all times during the day, ready for a hard response if it became necessary.

That was only for a real emergency, though. The kind that Ahoub, with all of his experience on the great river, couldn't handle. The others on the *Khufu* knew that Fang and his subordinates were mercenaries, but they didn't know about the heavy gear: *Paladin* and the combat suits for Fang, Travis and Laney. The gear stayed in the hold, until or unless it was needed.

Fang showed up and leaned against the railing next to her with his back to the water. "How's it feel to be the head honcho?"

Emily turned her head to look at the leader of Ghost Team. "You've been talking to Travis too much. You're starting to sound like a Texan."

Fang fixed her with his penetrating gaze. "You didn't answer the question."

"It's scary," Emily admitted.

"Good."

"Good?"

"You're smart enough to be scared." He shifted around so that, like her, he was looking out over the water. She wondered if the river affected him the way it did her. "As long as it doesn't paralyze you, fear is healthy. It makes you plan better and train harder. It makes you focus."

"I think Kushner plans too much, and takes too long doing it."

"And you think you'll be better?"

"Maybe." She smiled slightly. "I'm more adaptable, anyway." She tightened her grip on the railing until her knuckles turned white. "I just want to rescue the artwork, and not get anybody hurt in the process. I don't think Kushner really cares about the art."

Fang raised an eyebrow, which was easily the most expressive she'd seen him being during their brief acquaintance. "The art matters to you that much?"

"Yeah," Emily said. "You want the real reason I'm here?"

Fang nodded.

"You pulled out too early on the Clementine retrieval. Twenty-six priceless, irreplaceable paintings, probably lost to history forever."

Fang stared at her for a moment. "Kushner made the call," he said finally.

Emily shook her head. "It was a bad call." She stood silent for a moment, bemused as she watched a tree branch floating upstream. The Amazon was a tidal river, even here more than twelve hundred kilometers from the coast. Twice a day, the current reversed itself in seeming contradiction to the natural order of things. "I want this mission to succeed. The people who funded this mission put me on it, over Kushner's objections, to ensure its success."

Emily leaned on the railing and looked out across the water. "Second-in-command, and he wouldn't listen to a thing I said. We haven't gamed the operation at all. Hell, we don't even have a real backup plan for the extraction."

"Ghost Team does."

"Yay, teamwork. I'm loving all the fine-tuned..." Imitating Travis' Texas drawl, she said, "*...co-ord-i-nation.*" She rolled her eyes. "And I'll give you even odds that the Chinese are already onto this recovery opportunity. The Aggies, sorry, the AAG, their Antiquities and Acquisitions Group, are never far behind the Monumentalists."

"Let's get together to discuss—" Fang stopped in mid-sentence, obviously paying attention to something on Ghost Team's comm net. "Tell the captain there's a Chinese patrol boat up ahead around the bend. They will undoubtedly be coming aboard." Fang moved off at a fast jog.

That wasn't good. They were a UN-protected humanitarian mission, so the Chinese technically couldn't interfere with them without causing a diplomatic incident. On the other hand, if they had the guts to board and inspect *Khufu* anyway, they'd discover Ghost Team, *Paladin* and the *artistes*. End of mission, and a clear diplomatic win for the Chinese.

Ten minutes later, Emily was standing next to Captain Ahoub as a Chinese officer nimbly stepped down from the gunwale of the patrol boat, which was both larger and more heavily armed than their riverboat, to the deck of the *Khufu*, followed by two troopers. Emily wasn't sure what she'd expected, but the officer was a dapper thirty-something who greeted them with a smile and introduced himself as Lieutenant Commander Ye Jing.

Captain Ahoub handed Jing a packet containing the ship's papers and the travel pass issued by the United Nations. "Welcome to the *Khufu*, sir. I'm Captain Ahoub." He gestured at Emily. "And this is Emily Gravely, one of the organizers of our medical relief effort." That was her cover identity; ostensibly, she was a medical administrator.

Emily smiled at the Chinese officer and held out her hand.

Jing took her hand, but rather than shaking it, he bent and kissed it in the French style. Looking up at her with twinkling eyes, he said, "Ah, yes. One of the angels I've heard so much about. What do you think of Brazil, Miss Gravely?"

"Breathtakingly beautiful," she said, "and appallingly nightmarish, in equal measure."

He cocked his head. Pursing his lips, he said, "Then you have grasped the essence of modern Brazil. A beautiful land, marred by decades of warfare that has gutted entire generations and all but wrecked the country." He smiled. "Still, we'll be bringing all of that to an end shortly. It's amazing what can be accomplished with Chinese discipline."

Lieutenant Commander Jing looked down and gave a perfunctory glance at the package he'd been handed. He nodded at Captain Ahoub. "Sir, your papers are in order. I will not hinder your passage."

Well, that was a relief off Emily's mind. The mission could have easily ended right here.

Jing looked both of them in the eyes, in turn. "But I will humbly advise you not to proceed further. The river beyond this point is not a safe place." He looked away, the smile slipping from his face momentarily to reveal the world-weary countenance of a soldier who'd seen too many bad things. "There are river pirates, territorial warlords and, one hears, bands of predatory child soldiers. Perhaps even, how you say it, the Boogie Man." He turned back to face them. "This Guerra, whose very name mean 'War' in Portuguese."

"I take the relief mission where they need to go," Captain Ahoub replied.

The Chinese officer looked inquiringly at Emily.

"Would you say that there are more people in need of medical assistance ahead of us or behind us?"

"Ahead, assuredly," Jing answered, shaking his head sadly.

"Then that is where we are going."

Jing nodded. "I wish you well. It is a fine thing you all do, I just fear for your safety."

07. Back-Channel Communications

War Zone, 23:42
Amazon River, 111 km east of Manaus

Emily snuggled deeper into the bed.

"I was surprised when you knocked on my door." Ahoub nibbled her ear, eliciting a giggle from Emily. "Pleased, mind you, but still surprised."

He was lying next to her with his arm casually draped across her flat stomach and his head next to hers on the pillow. Smiling, she turned her head to look at him. His brown eyes were fixed on her face and his expression was uncharacteristically serious.

In the face of her silence, he caressed her cheek gently with his thumb. Finally, she said, "Just butterflies, I guess. The rendezvous is tomorrow." No backing out after tomorrow.

"And you're frightened?"

"Yes, of course," she said. "Who wouldn't be?" Once the mission team left the *Khufu*, they'd be on their own. And if anything went wrong, well, there were a lot of ways to die in a war zone.

"The artwork is that important to you?"

"Yes."

"Important enough for you to risk your life? I mean, you're a curator not a mercenary."

She turned and kissed him lightly. Pulling back a little, she said, "I've loved art, especially paintings, for as long as I can remember. I came by it naturally, I suppose. My father was a museum director and my mother was a graphic artist with a passion for Renaissance paintings. She'd always talk about famous paintings as if they were people, like they spoke to her, made her feel new emotions, showed her the world in different ways. Her favorite painting was the Mona Lisa, so one day I asked if I could see it."

"Oh."

"Yeah. I remember, she got this strange expression on her face. Then she told me that I could see a photo of it, but not the real thing. The real painting had been destroyed in the Paris Flash, when I was just a baby. I recall being devastated, like something beautiful, and profound, had been expunged from the world.

"Maybe it's stupid," Emily said, "but I can't let that happen, losing another important painting. Not when I can do something about it."

"Not stupid," Ahoub said gently. "Brave. Stubborn, for sure."

"Well, that's me. Stubborn is my middle name." She smiled. "What about you? How'd they twist your arm to make you take this mission?"

Ahoub was silent for a moment. At Emily's searching glance, he finally said, "Kushner really underestimated you, didn't he?"

She smiled. "Apparently."

"You know Kushner was Intelligence during the war, right?"

"No, I didn't. I knew he wasn't combat ops, though. Not that he'd ever admit that."

"His contacts got him some photos that, if circulated to the wrong people, could make some very powerful...factions...angry with me. Angry enough to make an example of me, no matter where I am on the river."

"Dare I ask..."

Ahoub reached over and cupped her cheek, then dropped his hand away. "About eight years ago, we were beset by raiders. They thought *Khufu* would be an easy, rich target, but we ripped them apart with the Tempest. By the time the shell casings stopped flying, we discovered that they'd been towing their last conquest." He frowned. "A slaveship. With a hold full of women destined for brothels throughout Brazil and beyond."

"What did you do?"

"We took them under tow. Found a UN peacekeeping encampment to drop them off at."

"How does that—"

"Kushner's got photos of us towing what is obviously a slave transport. Show them to one group of people, I look like a slaver. Show them to the slavers, I look like somebody who stole a lot of valuable merchandise from them. Either way, it's big trouble for me."

"I'm sorry," Emily said.

"Not your fault."

"If I can," she said, "I'll make those photos disappear." She sat up, a determined look on her face. "No matter what, Kushner won't be using anything against you after this, or I'll set the Fuzzy Pandas on him."

"You would do—"

"Of course," Emily responded. "Hell, the honest truth is we shouldn't even be piggybacking on a humanitarian mission like this one. Historically, it's a bad idea. When it comes out, and it *always* comes out eventually, it makes everyone distrust the very people who are trying to make things better."

He gathered her into his arms and held her.

After a short time, Ahoub asked, "Is the artwork really that valuable?"

Emily smiled. "Yeah. A couple billion creds. At least."

His eyes widened. "So, a high value target. And highly disposable on the black market?"

"Yeah, if you know what you're doing. Ironically, the Batista's inquiries are what led us to them."

"I don't like it." He shook his head. "So you can't guarantee that you're the only ones that know about the artwork?"

"No." She paused. "In fact, I'm worried about one group in particular. If anybody's going to be a problem, I'd put money down on the Aggies."

"Even worse, then. Could be a free-for-many." He cocked his head. "That's the American expression, right?"

"Free-for-all," Emily corrected.

"Ah, yes. Free-for-all." Ahoub sat up. "You should leave."

She gaped at him. "What?"

"Get some rest. Take a pill if you have to." He paused. "Look, I know this thing we're having is a fling, but I'd like to see you again. If you want to survive this, you need to focus. From now until it's over, no distractions, just...focus. And if it all falls apart, run for your life. I have a contact in Manaus who might be able to help you."

She got up and started putting her clothes on. She heard him get off the bed.

A moment later, he handed her a slip of paper with a name and an address on it. "Memorize it. Then burn it."

"OK," Emily said, heading for the door. She grabbed the doorknob, then turned back to look at him. The light beyond the bed highlighted his chiseled physique.

He said gently, "Stay safe, Em."

"You, too."

"Don't worry about me," Ahoub said, smiling widely. "If I see trouble coming, I'm running."

DAY 4

The Gulf Stream, by Winslow Homer, 1899. Oil on canvas. OWU Catalog #6.

An exhausted man lies on the deck of a dismasted, rudderless fishing boat, while threatened by sharks and a distant waterspout. He is oblivious to the schooner visible on the horizon behind him, which portends a potential rescue.

The painting is based on sketches and watercolors Homer created during several trips to the Bahamas. Painted shortly after the death of his father in 1898, some have interpreted the painting as an expression of the artist's sense of mortality.

08. Separation

War Zone, 13:07
Amazon River, 95 km east of Manaus

"Kushner wants to talk to you."

Emily stopped giving directions to the staff setting up for their latest stop and turned to face Ester, who looked up at her with big, unblinking eyes. She'd heard that Kushner had finally regained consciousness earlier in the morning, but frankly didn't particularly want to talk with him.

She nodded and followed Ester to Kushner's cabin. Gwyn Chambers was waiting for them outside when they arrived.

"Put these on before you go in," the doctor said, handing them all blue surgical masks. "Believe me, you don't want to catch what he's got." After they'd donned the masks, the doctor opened the door for them, but stayed outside. "Try not to tire him out. I'd like my patient to survive this trip."

Kushner was lying on his narrow bunk as they filed in, a bony outline underneath a beige blanket. He was sweating despite the chill of the air conditioning. He'd lost weight since Emily had least seen him and looked at least ten years older.

"There's no way I can go on the mission," Kushner said. Whatever he was going to say next was aborted as he succumbed to an extended bout of coughing.

Ester stepped in smoothly. "He's dictated some instructions he wants you to follow—"

"I don't care what he wants," Emily said flatly. "I'm in charge now. We'll carry out the mission as best we can, but we'll adapt as necessary."

"You'll follow my instructions," Kushner said, almost, but not quite, smiling. "Or face the consequences later." Sick as a dog, but still reveling in confronting the woman who'd been shoved onto his mission by his political enemies.

"You don't get it." Emily smiled with fake sweetness. "All this," she said, gesturing airily. "I don't care about the glory. You can have all the credit. You can even make me the scapegoat if the mission fails. All I want to do is rescue the paintings."

Ester said, "You don't even have any military experience."

Emily chuckled, which was probably a little mean, but it was enervating to not have to tiptoe around Kushner's giant ego. "Neither does Kushner, really. Not tactical, anyway. That's what we have Ghost Team for."

She saw Kushner bridle at that, but he suffered another fit of coughing before he could get a word out. Yes, Kushner had served in the military during the Time of Troubles, as the historians euphemistically called it. So had just about every man, and lots of women, in his age group. He'd even been in combat zones, just never when fighting was actually going on, a fact she'd seen him carefully gloss over in conversations.

Kushner finally recovered from his coughing bout. "You don't have the grit to make the tough decisions—"

Emily snapped, "You mean, like the Clementine recovery, where you abandoned the prize?"

The former mission commander raised his voice, or tried to, but it came out raspy and only slightly louder. "You dare to critique me?"

Ester, ever the lackey, let loose a loud laugh. "You'd need a ladder to come up to his level."

Emily pursed her lips. "Screw you. Both of you. I don't need this bullshit, not right now." She headed for the door; she had to get away before she lost her temper.

Kushner said, "Cross me, and you still think that job at the Metropolitan is going to be waiting for you?"

With the door half open, Emily turned back to look at him. "Are you threatening me?" She cocked her head and frowned. "Aren't the Monumentalists a volunteer organization? Hell of a way to treat a volunteer."

She left the room.

War Zone, 14:46
Amazon River, 84 km east of Manaus

"Hey, Ophelia," Emily said, climbing down into *Paladin's* interior. She was pleased to see that Ophelia was the only one in the APC.

"Hey, yourself," Ophelia responded, turning around and smiling. "What's up?"

Emily sat down at the fire control station, across from Ophelia's seat. "I've got something kind of confidential for you." Ophelia arched an eyebrow. "Ahoub gave me a contact in Manaus, in case everything goes bad."

"Oh."

"I'm not sure I see any real scenario where we'd need it, but I think Ghost Team should have it, too. I just…don't want it to be…common knowledge. Not unless it's needed."

"Kind of like: In case of emergency, break glass?"

"Yeah. Like that."

"I can do that."

War Zone, 23:38
Amazon River, 68 km east of Manaus

Sanford and three other members of the *artistes* were already gathered by the still closed door of the cargo hold when Emily arrived, all with hefty black duffel bags carrying their clothes and other belongings. The surprise was that Ester was with them.

As soon as the diminutive woman spotted Emily, she started forward, an angry and determined look on her face. “Why did you tell them they might not be coming back to the ship?”

“First of all,” Emily said mildly. “I don’t answer to you.” She cocked her head and looked down at Ester. “Second, if anybody’s on to us at all, they’ll be expecting us to smuggle the artwork out on the *Khufu.* It’s the obvious choice. I don’t like being obvious.”

“But Steven said—”

“He’s not in charge anymore.”

Ester insisted, “That doesn’t give you the right to change the plan.”

Emily gawked at her. “Um, yes, it does.” It seemed to her that Kushner’s assistant was having a little difficulty processing the changed circumstances.

She heard the door open and looked over to see Travis beckoning them all into the hold. They filed past the mercenary, Ester tagging behind them. The group advanced about five meters and then, almost as if via some shared unconscious impulse, stopped and spread out to look at the APC glistening under the spotlights. It looked sleek and dangerous, especially with its main gun starkly silhouetted.

She was gratified to see that they’d changed the *Paladin’s* coloring back to its default jungle camouflage pattern.

While they were collectively studying their next mode of transport, she managed to catch Sanford's eye. Under her withering glare, he gave her a look of chagrin and a modest shrug.

Fair enough. Even Sanford probably had some difficulties handling someone like Ester. She'd probably forgive him for letting her tag along sometime in the next century. Maybe.

Laney emerged from the open personnel compartment at the back of the APC and waved at them. At the same time, she heard footsteps and low voices behind her as more people walked into the hold. Turning, she found Captain Ahoub accompanied by Miller and her last artiste, who was plaintively apologizing for having overslept.

"The gang's all here," Travis said, closing the door. "Time to get this rodeo started."

While Laney helped get everyone settled into the APC, Emily followed Ahoub over to a metal cabinet on the wall of the hold.

"Are you ready?" he asked.

She shrugged. "As ready as I'll ever be."

He chuckled.

Turning, he pressed his thumb against a marked square on the cabinet. There was a hum as it opened and a two-handed control rig unfolded itself from inside the compartment. Ahoub grabbed the controls. Moments later, what Emily had assumed were steel beams along the ceiling of the hold started moving and Emily realized she was looking at a cargo gantry. As she watched, a rectangular lift harness settled into place a few meters above the APC.

Four cables descended from the harness. Travis took each one in turn and attached it to hooks on the underside of the APC.

"Time for you to go, Em," Ahoub said softly. "And good luck. Remember, I want to see you again after all this is done."

"I know," Emily said, grinning. She added more softly, "Me, too." Using her body to block the view from *Paladin*, she reached over and held his hand for a moment, before turning away.

Walking over to the APC, she found everybody belted into the APC's barebones seats, with their duffels already stored behind some netting. Except for her own bag, which Laney wordlessly took from her and stowed.

The only incongruous note was Ester, belted in next to the others, who looked up at her defiantly. "I'm coming along."

"No, you're not, Ester." She had no skills or experience that Emily needed on the excursion and, frankly, she didn't need the disruption. In a vain attempt to soften the blow, she said, "I appreciate your willingness, but this isn't really for you. I'm sorry." Ester looked away, clearly not intending to move.

Travis said, "Miss Ester, you can either get up or I'll pick you up and remove you."

Ester looked up at the mercenary. Something in his face must have convinced her that he was telling the truth about forcibly removing her. She undid her seatbelt, stood up without a word and stalked away, chin clenched and shoulders stiff with anger.

Travis gave Emily a glance that she couldn't read. As soon as Ester stepped off the APC's ramp, he engaged the controls to close up the APC. Emily quickly sat down and attached her own seatbelt. Moments later, the APC was suspended in the air.

While she couldn't see it, she knew what was happening. Part of the hold was covered by a false floor, one that Ahoub was now sliding out of the way to reveal an underwater hatch just a bit larger than the APC. He'd be opening the hatch momentarily.

As expected, a minute or two later, Emily felt the APC move slightly as Ahoub positioned it over the hatch. She could feel the vehicle swinging from side to side. She figured Ahoub was probably waiting for the swings to dampen out. After another minute or so, they started to descend.

"Our feet are wet," Armel, Ghost Team's APC driver, called out loudly enough to be heard in the personnel compartment.

With a gentle thud, *Paladin* settled on the river bottom at a slight angle. A few seconds later, there was a series of thumps as Armel did something to release the cables.

Paladin started rolling along the bottom, leaving *Khufu* behind them.

DAY 5

The Chess Players, by Thomas Eakins, 1876. Oil on wood. OWU Catalog #114.

The artist's father, Benjamin Eakins, watches a chess game in the parlor of an elegant Philadelphia home. The painting features vibrant colors, careful spatial construction and meticulous detail. Chess aficionados will also note that White, on the left side, is distinctly at a disadvantage in the endgame.

In 1881, the painting was the first work of art to be accepted by the Metropolitan Museum of Art as a gift from a living artist.

09. RENDEZVOUS

War Zone, 8:07
Amazon River, 68 km east of Manaus

Gwyn Chambers slipped into her cabin, then knelt to root around in one of her suitcases. She pulled out a smooth, black ovoid about five centimeters long.

Holding the ovoid up to her lips, she said, "Is anybody—"

"We're listening." The voice was in English, but with a Chinese accent.

"They're not here," Gwyn said. "They left the ship sometime in the middle of the night."

"How?"

"I don't know. I didn't see them leave. I know where they're going, though."

"And that is?"

"Manaus. They're recovering some missing artwork. I overheard a conversation."

"Do you have any details on Kushner's timeline?"

"No, but Kushner's not with them," Gwyn said. "He's out of commission. Picked up a nasty bug." She still wondered whether Kushner was just unlucky, which was possible, or whether somebody had deliberately infected him. "His second in command, Emily Gravely, is in charge now."

"Interesting."

"Is...is my brother OK?" Her brother was a human rights activist and had been captured by the Chinese while engaged in illegal activities.

"Yes, of course." There was the barest hint of a chuckle from the speaker. "Gwyn, this is not a Tri-D show. We are civilized people. Would you like to speak with him?"

"Yes, please."

War Zone, 9:31
Amazon River, 42 km east of Manaus

Emily stood behind Ophelia, holding on tightly to the back of Ophelia's chair as Armel piloted *Paladin* along the river bottom. The APC was having no significant problems navigating the muddy terrain, though Armel's talents were clearly on display, but the ride was far from comfortable for the passengers. Despite the steady, powerful flow of the river, a surprising amount of debris collected on the bottom and *Paladin* couldn't always go around it.

"Gregorio, come in," Ophelia said. "Can you read me?" Ghost Team's EWS was relaying a signal through one of her drones, trying to reach the local contact who'd be helping them get into Manaus.

They'd been searching for quite a while. Emily figured he'd done his best to hide overnight. The river was a dangerous place.

"*Oi! Born dia!*" a voice boomed in Portuguese. "*About time you all showed up. I was gettin' real lonesome.*"

Emily smiled, then looked to the side and saw Fang watching her. "Hey, time for the next stage," she said.

"Indeed," Fang replied.

Ophelia and Gregorio Ruiz exchanged GPS coordinates and worked out their respective positions. About thirty minutes later, *Paladin* came to a stop below Gregorio's boat, a dilapidated craft about fifteen meters long anchored beneath several looming trees that overhung the river. Armel positioned them so they could do the personnel transfer on the shoreward side of the boat, under the shelter of the trees to subvert possible satellite observation.

Armel deployed an Egress Tube, Retractable, or ETR; basically, a tube with a built-in ladder and flotation arranged around the opening up top. Laney, in her combat suit, went up the tube first, then Emily and her team followed, one by one. Their contact had hung a rope ladder off the side of his boat, so they were able to get aboard relatively easily.

Finding room to stand on the deck was a bit harder. The deck was covered with wooden boxes, baskets of vegetables, and various odds and ends. It looked like what it really was, a working cargo ship.

Gregorio Ruiz turned out to be a sixtyish, dark-skinned Brazilian with a wide smile, a wizened face and graying hair.

He took one look at Laney in her combat suit, cocked his head, and asked, "How do you pee?"

"You don't even want to know."

He grinned and looked around at his passengers. "So which one of you is Kushner?"

Emily stepped forward. "Kushner got sick, so I'm in charge. I'm Emily Gravely." She held her hand out.

Gregorio shook her hand. "Are you nicer than him?"

"God, I hope so." She laughed. "It'd be hard to be more of a jerk." There was some muttered agreement from the rest of her team, which caused Gregorio to raise an eyebrow.

"Well," he said, stepping back and patting the structure behind him, "this here is your cargo container. We rebuilt the aft section of the deckhouse around it." Emily raised an eyebrow. If that was rebuilt then Gregorio's people had done an excellent job of making the alterations as shabby-looking as the rest of the boat. "Right now, it's full of stuff we're taking to Manaus, just like all the deck cargo."

Emily gave him a quizzical look.

He shrugged. "You can't go to the city with an empty boat and not be noticed." It seemed to Emily that Gregorio had just saved them from one of Kushner's planning mistakes.

War Zone, 11:36
Bang Hai, 483 km east of Manaus

"We found them. Ninety-five percent likelihood, according to the analysts."

"Excellent news."

"They're in a small cargo craft, looks like they're carrying a real cargo to blend in. They'll most likely arrive later this afternoon, sell the cargo and then wait around until they can start their recovery run."

"So, we could intercept them?"

"Yes, sir."

"But we don't have definitive coordinates for where the paintings are?"

"No, sir. We know they're in Manaus, but not exactly where."

"Well, the Monumentalists obviously have a plan. We'll let them get the paintings, then we'll just...take them."

"Shouldn't be a problem, sir." Before his commander could leave, he added, "By the way, we identified their mercs. They call themselves Ghost Team." He put a slightly blurry photo of the team's leader on the screen.

"They're led by a deserter from our Special Ops."

"Interesting. Well, then, we shouldn't have any trouble getting Special Ops involved, if we need them."

10. Interference

War Zone, 13:12
Amazon River, 23 km east of Manaus

Ophelia leaned back in her chair and groaned as something in her back cracked. She tried doing some light stretches to ease her aches and pains. General Dynamics had put a surprising amount of effort into making the APC's chairs comfortable, but no chair was up to the number of hours she spent in front of her screens.

She leaned forward as one of her drones showed three boats approaching from upstream.

"We've got incoming," she said over Ghost Team's encrypted comms channel. "Three boats, decent condition, no markings. Coming downriver toward us. Designating as contact Alpha."

She quickly got an "*Understood, moving into position,*" from Laney and a quiet "*Got it,*" from Emily, who was tied into their network now.

"Looks like the *artistes* have picked up some fleas," Travis observed, sitting at the fire control station behind Armel.

"Close up the distance," Fang commanded, "and tell the boat to slow down." The boat had been keeping their speed down to match the APC's slower pace, but they were still about two hundred meters ahead of them. *Paladin* surged forward as Armel complied. The ride got noticeably rougher.

Ophelia relayed the message to Emily on the boat, then got a drone into position to get a closer view of the approaching force. The boats were full of armed men, perhaps twenty in all, carrying rifles, machine guns and pistols. No heavy weaponry that she could see. The boats looked like gasoline/alcohol conversion jobs, probably underpowered but serviceable. They were clearly pirates, and brazen ones at that, to be working so close to Manaus. Either that, or the Batista influence was severely waning in anticipation of the upcoming Chinese push.

Fang looked over at Ophelia. "They must have a spotter. Find him and take him out."

"On it," she said.

"Travis," Fang said. "Prepare to fire antipersonnel rounds."

Travis shot him an over-the-shoulder look to make sure he was serious. "You got it." Antipersonnel rounds were intended to take out combat-suited soldiers en masse. Against wooden boats, the results were going to be ugly.

War Zone, 13:18
Amazon River, 23 km east of Manaus

Emily was in the boat's small bridge with Gregorio when she got the warning from Ghost Team that trouble was in the offing. She relayed Fang's order to slow down to Gregorio, who instantly complied, then sent an alert to her team and made sure they were all safely gathered in the cramped common room behind the craft's small bridge—cramped mostly because of all the space taken up to accommodate their cargo container.

"Three boats, pirates, coming downstream," Emily explained. "Ghost Team's going to take care of them."

Gregorio raised an eyebrow.

Emily shrugged. "Don't ask me, I don't know how they're going to handle this."

Through the bridge's window, Emily saw a shimmering haze moving across the deck, then realized after a moment that it was Laney, dynamic camouflage engaged, taking up a position at the bow. It was hard to tell, but she thought the mercenary may have gone prone on the deck. Assuming she had a weapon deployed, it must have been camouflaged, too.

"*COB, maintain course,*" Ophelia said. COB was her own codename, which Fang had told her meant Commander of Boat. Apparently, Ghost Team had found it humorous to apply the term to a civilian like herself with no naval or other military experience. "*And get your heads down, it's about to get dangerous.*"

Emily knelt. Gregorio looked down at her, got the hint and joined her on the floor, though he did keep a hand on the bottom of the wheel to keep the boat steady on its course. In a sensorium window, she flipped through Ophelia's working list of key drone views until she found one that showed their boat and surrounding area from above.

"*Spotter is down,*" Ophelia said.

Emily watched as the three pirate boats rounded a bend in the river. Two of them sped up when they spotted their target. Emily heard gunfire, realized that the pirates had fired warning shots past their boat.

Beneath the seemingly peaceful water, Travis targeted three brilliant antipersonnel rounds, one at each boat. Each round was effectively a miniature missile with enough built-in smarts to determine the best way to engage its designated target. A primary mandate of their targeting instructions included not damaging a nearby wooden craft designated as "friendly." Designed for both underwater and aerial use, each round determined the amount of propellant that needed to be expended to reach the target and penetrate the hull.

What Emily witnessed was the first two boats simply disintegrating, followed a few seconds later by the third. Splinters of wood, body parts, engine pieces and structural elements flew into the air, accompanied by flame and smoke as the fuel supplies caught fire.

A few lucky survivors suddenly found themselves unexpectedly in the water. Then Emily heard the staccato *boom-boom-boom* of nearby rifle fire, and realized that the men in the water weren't so lucky after all, as Laney targeted them.

A moment later, Ophelia said, "*Alpha force has been squashed. You're clear to proceed, just try to stay away from the debris.*"

Emily stood up and Gregorio followed suit. Where three boats had been, there was only scattered wreckage. Even the fires were burning themselves out.

"*The only good pirate is a dead pirate,*" Laney said, satisfaction in her voice.

Emily had no particular sympathy for pirates who'd undoubtedly harmed a lot of innocent people, but it shocked even her, and she'd witnessed it via drone view, that twenty bloodthirsty pirates could meet a violent end so quickly. It was the very definition of an asymmetric fight, amateurs against seasoned mercenaries with top-of-the-line equipment.

Gregorio watched the wreckage as it drifted downstream past them. He turned to her and said, "I'm glad you're on my side." He shuddered. "I'd hate to end that way."

War Zone, 14:33
Amazon River, 6 km east of Manaus

A little more than an hour after their ill-fated encounter with the pirates, Gregorio turned to Emily with a wide grin. "Welcome to the Meeting of the Waters."

She looked up from her flexxi, with its fold-out digital screen, on which she'd been studying the One World United Exhibition manifest for the umpteenth time. Gregorio had the boat near the middle of the river, so it was easy to see the famously divided waters downstream from the mighty waterway's juncture with the Rio Negro. Despite the inexorable merging of their flows, the rivers refused to give up their identities, the dark, turgid waters of the Rio Negro running alongside the light-colored, sediment-heavy Amazon waters for kilometers, a byproduct of differences in temperature, sediment load, density or, perhaps, just sheer anthropomorphic stubbornness.

Manaus was close.

RECOVERY OP

The Harvesters, by Pieter Bruegel the Elder, 1565. Oil on wood. OWU Catalog #60.

A depiction of the everyday life of peasants at the end of a hot summer workday in the Netherlands. Workers picnic and relax after their hard labor in the golden fields.

Part of a set of six (with only five surviving) paintings commissioned by Antwerp merchant Niclaes Jongelinck for his home. Bruegel's series is a watershed moment in Western art, favoring a new humanism over previously dominant religious themes.

11. Approach

Cargo Boat, 01:22

A half-moon shone in the dark sky as a decrepit cargo boat, its running lights conspicuously off, chugged its way carefully through the narrow waterways of the *favela* that had grown up where the Amazon encroached on the city of Manaus. Even here, more than fourteen hundred kilometers from the coast, the Amazon was a tidal river; it was the high tide that had made the boat's surreptitious course possible, and also bounded its use as an escape route.

In the narrower places, the fifteen-meter-long craft almost touched the ramshackle buildings and walkways. A determined resident could have stepped onto the boat, had they not been discouraged by the men stationed on either side of the boat with machine guns.

Inside the boat, the brightly-lit bridge provided a stark contrast to the boat's external appearance, the illumination invisible from outside thanks to the recently installed one-way windows. Emily sat next to Gregorio, who was helping them navigate their way as discreetly as possible to the warehouse district that was their destination. She was wearing a headset with an attached mic and frowning at the foldout screen in front of her.

"Left up ahead. Then slow down some more 'cause the next turn is going to be a squeaker."

Gregorio nodded. "What's this all about, anyway?" Turning, he gave her a gap-toothed grin. "If you're allowed to tell me." He'd been very well paid, so technically she didn't have to tell him squat. In addition to money, his deal had also included getting his extended family out of war-torn Brazil. On the other hand, the mission was in progress and the need for operational security was past.

Emily smiled back at him. "Artwork."

Gregorio raised his eyebrows. "Artwork?" He turned away to concentrate on navigating the "squeaker" that Emily had mentioned, his hands moving the steering wheel in minute increments.

On her screen, Emily looked at an aerial view from the drone that Ophelia had stationed above them. Thanks to Gregorio's expert handling, the boat made the turn with about a foot to spare on each side.

In her ear phones, Ophelia said, "*COB, continue down the channel. Ghost Team is almost in place.*" The drone operator was back on *Paladin*, which was submerged just outside of Manaus.

"Paintings," Emily said. "Thirty-two years ago, in 2082, the One World United Art Exhibition was in Brazil when the war started. It disappeared, nobody knew who stole it." She looked over at Gregorio. "Well, it's just surfaced here in Manaus and we're taking it back. Tonight."

"So, you're stealing back your own stolen paintings?"

"Yes."

"I like it."

"*Ghost One is in position.*" She recognized the clipped tones and Chinese accent of Fang Li, the leader of Ghost Team.

Warehouse Complex (Back Gate), 01:23

Laney Sanders, Ghost Three, let the Diver Propulsion Vehicle pull her slowly through the murky and badly polluted water. The DPV was shaped like a three-foot-long missile with a propeller on the back end, safely encased in a wire cage to avoid unfortunate incidents. Laney gripped the handles that extended from each side of the propeller cage. She toggled the DPV to a slower speed as she spotted obstacles looming up out of the muck in front of her.

The view wasn't real, of course. It was a composite extrapolated from her suit's various sensors, including the stealth sonar rig they'd added for this mission, and projected on her face screen by her suit's AI. Without it, she'd have been swimming blind.

She was moving through the open area of water that separated the rear of the warehouse complex from the rest of the *favela*. Based on the wreckage she was seeing, mostly broken timbers and smashed furniture, the open area had probably been created by simply destroying the homes of any residents who had been unlucky enough to be living too close to the complex. Recent regimes had been brutal.

Whoever owned the warehouses had upgraded the security by adding a ten-foot spiked fence, topped with razorwire, around the entire complex. In their zeal, they'd extended the fence into the water, with the help of an improbable amount of underwater concrete. Of course, they'd included a gate to allow authorized boats access to the loading dock.

She reached the gate just as she heard Fang Li announce that he was in position, followed a moment later by Trav, Ghost Two.

"Ghost Three, in position," she said.

Cargo Boat, 01:24

Emily split her screen into quarters, showing the helmet view of each member of Ghost Team, plus an enhanced overhead view of the complex that Ophelia was providing from her drones. On the overhead view, the three team members were green dots, each one in their designated positions.

Emily's mouth was dry and her stomach felt queasy. This was the one part of the mission over which she had no control and no expertise. It was almost surreal that she was in charge—she was an art historian, not a military commander.

Ophelia said, "*Infrared shows zeds, locations as follows.*"

A bunch of red dots appeared on the strategic view. One looked like it was in the gatehouse at the front of the complex, as expected. Another was in their target warehouse. Then there was a cluster of six red dots in one of the other warehouses, gathered in approximately a circle.

She frowned. That seemed odd. There was supposed to be one guard per building. Why were so many of them in one place?

From Fang Li, allocating objectives: "*One, gatehouse, then open backdoor; Two, take the cluster; Three, secure the backdoor then the target.*"

"*Two, cluster, affirmative.*"

"*Three, backdoor and target, affirmative.*"

Ophelia said, "*The weather is still clear.*"

Emily shook her head and smiled. Ophelia was even worse at military-style radio-speak than she was. That was apparently her way of saying that her eyeballs hadn't detected any threats,

She leaned forward. "Mission is 'go.'" She felt just a little bit helpless, not a comfortable feeling for somebody as detail-oriented as herself. Now it was completely up to Ghost Team.

Fang responded, "*Confirmed. Go.*"

On her screen, the little green dots started moving.

12. Clear & Control

Warehouse Complex (Front Gate), 01:28

Fang Li, Ghost One, walked slowly up to the gatehouse, careful not to move faster than the chameleon capabilities of his suit could compensate for. He was sweating a little. He was walking across a minefield, which was always destined to be nerve-racking, even if the minefield was only activated if the guard on duty detected a threat. Fortunately, the guard not only wasn't looking at his external view screens (which wouldn't have shown anything, anyway), he had his head down and there seemed to be a bluish light shining up on his face from something he was holding. Fang was willing to bet he was playing some sort of electronic game.

The defenses included a regular infrared scan of the area, but his combat suit was currently in anti-infrared mode. He wasn't emitting anything hotter than the ambient temperature. While his suit couldn't store generated heat for long, this was exactly the type of situation for which the feature had been designed.

Fang's sensors indicated no other security mechanisms in play. As far as he could tell, the only significant defense that the stolen cache of paintings had was that, until tonight, nobody outside of a select few in the Batistas had known even remotely where the cache might be. Stolen paintings worth billions of creds, and nothing but security through obscurity. Unbelievable. Even worse, with all the bombing that the city had endured, it was a wonder that the warehouse complex had never been bombed.

Arriving at the guardhouse, Fang pointed his Marauder pistol at the window and blew a hole in the bulletproof glass with an UltraShock round. The guard gave a startled shout, dropped his ancient comms device and tried to stand up. Fang put the barrel of the weapon in the fist-sized hole and hit him with a tranquilizer round. He went down with a strangled scream and was still.

It was the work of seconds to smash the lock on the gatehouse door. He stepped over the comatose guard and looked at the control panel for a moment. Then he opened the back gate of the warehouse complex.

"Ghost One, the zed is down and the back door is open."

Puzzling over the controls again, Fang finally figured out how to turn the minefield on. He smiled. A nice surprise in case any unwelcome guests showed up at the front gate.

Warehouse Complex (Bldg. 4), 01:30

Travis McCloud, Ghost Two, had already infiltrated the complex and was standing outside the warehouse containing the cluster of guards pinpointed by Ophelia's drones. A fourteen-foot spiked fence was not an obstacle for a man in an elite combat suit.

He'd been waiting for Fang to take out the gatehouse, so that his own activities couldn't possibly alert the gatehouse guard and spoil Ghost One's stealthy approach. As soon as he heard that Fang had achieved his objectives, he entered the unlocked door of the warehouse.

Inside, the floor space was organized with wide floor-to-ceiling shelves separated by narrow aisles. Travis could see a yellow glow beyond all the shelving. He padded quietly down an aisle.

The guards were sitting about fifteen feet away at a makeshift table composed of a wide piece of plywood sitting on top of two sawhorses. They were playing some sort of card game.

Travis strolled around the corner, pistol up. One of the card players looked startled; he must have noticed a ripple of movement. He shot that guard first, then methodically shot the other guards. Accuracy was almost always better than speed. Only one even came close to getting his firearm out of its holster.

Warehouse Complex (Back Gate), 01:32

Laney swam to one side as the massive steel gate, the backdoor as Fang had called it, began to open. She waited until the gate was fully open, then triggered the ring-like packages she'd installed around the immense hinges.

Her screen dampened the brightness as chemicals mixed and flash-welded the hinges into position. Even through her suit, she felt a flash of heat as the steel melted together. Fang had told her before the mission that he liked to make sure his escape routes stayed open. Laney kind of agreed with his logic.

"Backdoor is locked open."

Laney engaged the DPV and headed for the muddy shore next to the dock. A moment later she turned it off, let go, and allowed the device's momentum to drive it a foot or so up onto the mud. She waited for a short interval to see if anybody started shooting in her general direction, though she didn't think that was likely. Still, in her experience, haste was a waste, unless you really needed it. She stood up in the now-thigh-deep water and trudged onto shore.

"*Cluster is down. It was six guards playing cards.*" Well, that was seven guards, including the one Fang had taken out, that would be sleeping until about noon tomorrow. How come Trav got most of the fun?

Her heads-up display showed her that stealth mode was engaging now that she'd left the water. You had to love the tech. Of course, she noted upon looking down, it didn't do much for muddy footprints.

She walked to the target warehouse's side door. Her display showed the guard as being somewhere on the other side of the building, so she grabbed the knob and turned it. She wasn't overly surprised to find it unlocked.

She stalked through a wide area filled with wooden boxes that looked suspiciously like they might hold paintings. Not exactly unexpected, but nice to see, nonetheless.

It turned out that her guard was in the bathroom.

She rolled her eyes.

After a short time, she heard a toilet flush. A moment later, a man emerged from the bathroom and she shot him with a tranquilizer round before he had a chance to even notice her.

"Target is secure," she said. "Bring in the *artistes*."

All her missions should be this easy.

13. First Contact

Warehouse Complex (Bldg. 6), 01:42

Emily jogged up to the warehouse's main entrance, now wide open, followed at a slower pace by her two art historians and the other volunteers with their rolling carts. A figure in a gray military combat suit stood by the door waiting for them. Too short to be Trav and too thin to be Fang, it had to be Laney.

As she drew abreast of the figure, her identification was confirmed when the fighter gave her a quick curtsy. She thought the suits looked vaguely unsettling, mostly due to their opaque facemasks.

Emily stopped next to Laney. "Well, the hard work can start now."

"Yeah, right," Laney drawled, accentuating her deep southern American accent. "You keep thinkin' that."

Emily laughed.

She spent the next ten minutes getting everybody organized. The first three boxes they opened were paintings, but they looked like local Brazilian artwork.

Valuable, but not what they were looking for. They set those to one side.

There were still a lot of boxes to look through, but the potential for disappointment was palpable. What if their information was wrong? They'd found paintings, and she'd bet her life savings that they were all stolen. But what if none of them were the stolen artwork they were hoping for?

Sanford, the more difficult and persnickety of her two art historians, called out, "We got one." She saw smiles break out on everyone's faces. Not a dry mission after all.

She rushed over to where Sanford was standing next to an empty box. It had three relatively small paintings in it, packed in the most dreadfully unprofessional way. Sanford carefully pulled out the middle one for her inspection.

"It's a Degas," he said, "from our list. It's *The Dancers*."

She high-fived him, then had to high-five some of the other workers that had come over to see the Monet, too.

Finally, she had to cut the impromptu celebration short. She stood on a chair and shouted, "All right, folks. We've got work to do. We can celebrate later." She paused. "And I've got a slight change of plans. No more inspections. We're just taking all of the paintings, including the Brazilian ones. So, let's get this show rolling."

When she stepped down from the chair, Sanford approached her. "All of them? Seriously?"

She'd figured he'd be the one to complain about her little change. He'd complained about so many other things already on this mission. She thought it was a good change, though. With this one adjustment, they not only saved the Brazilian paintings too, but they also reduced the time they needed to be in the warehouse. Listening to Ghost Team's activities on comms had reinforced for her that what they were doing was dangerous. She'd known that before, of course, but now she understood it for real.

"Yes, all of them. They're all stolen. And Brazil has a heritage that's worth preserving, too."

He looked at her intently, pursed his lips and nodded. "Good call." He turned around and walked away.

She spurred everybody on until there was a steady stream of boxes flowing back to the boat. Once they got a rhythm going, she was able to get a handle on how fast they were getting the job done, which was faster than her pre-mission estimates. By her calculation, it was going to take nearly an hour to get all of the boxes moved.

She walked over to Laney, still on station just inside the door.

"Most of the guards were playing cards, right?"

"Yes," Laney replied.

"How come this building's guard wasn't playing cards?"

"I don't know." Laney paused. "You're thinking he might have stayed here because he was expecting company tonight?"

"Yeah." Emily bit her lip, a bad habit that came out whenever she was stressed. "But it might just be me being nervous."

"In my experience, a little paranoia is a good thing."

"OK. If you don't think I'm crazy, then..." Emily keyed her mic. "Ophelia, we need a weather check. I've got a theory that our local guard might, emphasize might, have been expecting company sometime tonight."

Hawk APC, 02:08

Carlitos Paiva leaned back in his seat, rolled his eyes and tried to get comfortable, always a challenge while wearing a combat suit. On the encrypted command channel, relayed to his implants by the helmet resting on the floor of the APC next to his feet, General Diego had launched into yet another of his extended rants.

"Yes, we're still in transit," Carlitos Paiva said into the hand-held mic, trying to hide his irritation. He was the *expert*; you paid him to get stuff done, not to be micromanaged. "We'll be on station in thirty."

Paiva glanced at the wide, curved screen in front of him. An aerial drone view showed his convoy moving through the twisting, narrow streets of the *favela*. Not for the first time, he marveled at the stupidity of putting a warehouse complex in the section of the city with the worst roads, not to mention that half of the damn area was typically underwater. On the other hand, an area as devoid of useful infrastructure as the *favela* hadn't been pummeled by the extensive bombing that opposition forces, mostly their Chinese allies, had delivered to the rest of the city.

He had two troop carriers, followed by an eighteen-wheeler for cargo, plus a trailing gun truck. And his own Russian surplus APC in the fourth position—sleek, black and dangerous-looking. All to pick up his employer's retirement package, a billion-plus creds worth of stolen paintings, and provide security for it.

"You know how important this is. Don't fail me." General Diego terminated the call with a click. The tension in his employer's voice was obvious to Paiva; the man might be a fat, corrupt, womanizing slob but you had to give him some credit: he focused on details like nobody's business. He was probably the main reason the Batistas still held the city of Manaus.

Sadly, the man's compatriots were nowhere near as effective, which mostly explained why their faction was being pushed back by the Chinese-backed Nacionalistas. The fact that the rest of them generally ignored Paiva's military advice probably had a lot to do with it, too. Why hire a military advisor if you're not going to listen to him?

He turned toward Raynald, a thin, balding man perched like some maniacal spider in front of a wall of aerial views, real-time charts and windows with arcane technical gibberish scrolling past. "Anything? Our employer is getting nervous."

"Nah. Looks good. The drones aren't picking up anything interesting."

"Push the perimeter, please." Paiva scratched his scalp under his close-cropped black hair and grimaced. "I don't want any surprises."

"OK, boss."

Warehouse Complex (Bldg. 6), 02:16

Emily looked around with satisfaction. The inside of the warehouse appeared to be in total chaos, but it was actually an organized, functional maelstrom of activity. Basically, she'd orchestrated an assembly line, with several men moving crates into a staging area by the door, where another team of laborers would pick them up and move them to the boat. Her two art historians were in the boat arranging the boxes in storage as they arrived.

And Ghost Team, of course, was stationed outside to watch for trouble.

To her surprise, despite the precarious nature of their situation, she was enjoying herself. It felt like she was really accomplishing something here. Maybe it wasn't rescuing the Mona Lisa, but it was still something.

"*Problem,*" Ophelia said. "*Unknown drone just entered our ops space. I went to passive on that side of my detection envelope and low profile on everything else. Don't know if I was spotted.*"

Emily didn't need to be a military genius to realize this was bad. First, someone was probably coming here, just as she'd feared. Second, drones weren't regular issue for

Batista military units. So this unit was better equipped, and potentially better run, than regular Brazilian troops.

Fang said, "*Get a Midnight Special on station.*" Emily wasn't going to second-guess her combat specialist, but an electro-magnetic pulse seemed a little extreme, even the mini-EMP that Ghost Team had brought along. And it was going to take at least a few minutes to get here; *Paladin* was outside the city.

"*Roger that,*" Ophelia responded. "*Kind of expensive, though.*"

"*Ain't expensive, if you need it,*" Travis, Ghost Two, commented, chuckling. "*Plus, we can just add it to our bill.*"

"*Cut the chatter,*" Fang commanded. "*COB, recommend speeding up the recovery.*"

"Agreed." Emily looked around at all the activity and estimated the number of boxes still left in the warehouse. "Twenty minutes, minimum." Even at that, they were going to have to cut some serious corners.

There had always been risk associated with their mission, but now the enormity of her responsibilities hit home. These were her people. Hers. It was her job to make sure everyone got home safe. And that included Ghost Team, too.

Fang again. "*Ghost Two, seed the land approach as defined in Plan B, Option Two.*"

"*Boy, howdy, this is gonna be fun.*"

She turned and watched her crew working for a moment, all of them unaware of the complication headed their way.

"Listen up," she shouted. "We need to speed things up! I need everybody moving boxes NOW!"

14. First Strike

Hawk APC, 02:23

"Hey, Boss," Raynald called out. "Thought I saw something, but now it's gone."

Paiva cocked his head. Frowning, he considered his drone tech. He'd worked with Raynald for a long time. And if his tech thought he'd seen something, however briefly, then it was time to start worrying.

He didn't like surprises.

"Speculate, please."

"Felt like we just brushed up against somebody else's sensor envelope."

Paiva's eyebrows went up. "Somebody else with drones? Like ours?"

"Yeah." Even Sheffield, the APC's driver, looked up at that.

Their drones were state-of-the-art: six-centimeter, air-propelled globes filled with sophisticated electronics and sensors. Paiva knew this, both because he paid the bills, and because he regularly navigated the labyrinthine back channels necessary to procure the top-shelf mil-grade gear. The Batistas had been through too many years of war, and were too cash-strapped, to have that kind of gear. Which left either the Chinese or a third party. Either was very bad news.

"Well," he said, "That's not good." Keying his mic to the general convoy channel: "Pick up the pace, we may have a problem at our destination."

He placed a call to the gatehouse of the warehouse complex. There was no answer.

"Ray..."

"Already on it, boss. I'm pushing our perimeter out and I've released more—"

There was a flash, most of Raynald's screens went blank and the drone tech started cursing in a way Paiva hadn't heard from him in years. At the same time, Sheffield slammed on the brakes as the cargo vehicle in front of him coasted to a stop.

Still muttering under his breath, Raynald swiveled his chair around. He took a few seconds to compose himself. "We got hit with a mini-EMP. I just lost most of my drones."

Paiva whistled. Somebody had some *nice* toys.

Sheffield glanced over his Shoulder. "The cargo truck is down, too."

Well, that was going to put a crimp in their pickup schedule. *Memo to self: don't let General Diego requisition commercial vehicles for a mission again.*

Somebody had also just made a *lot* of noise. Not particularly dangerous to people, the mini-EMP had probably just fried everything electronic for a few blocks around them. Paiva suspected he'd be hearing from his employer again pretty soon.

The drones were combat-hardened as much as possible, but there was only so much you could do with a tiny, glorified instrument package that needed to float in the air. Close proximity to a mini-EMP wasn't survivable, though some on the opposite edge of the perimeter had survived. They carried more, but it was a finite and expensive supply.

Paiva made a snap judgment that this wasn't a full-on ambush, just a delaying tactic from a small force that had somehow beaten them to the warehouse complex. If he was wrong, he'd find out very soon.

"Squad One, dismount your team and take cover," Paiva said. Regular troop comms had been knocked out, but his own mercenaries were unaffected. He had three of his combat-suited soldiers with the first troop carrier, plus two more with the second team. "Squad Two, retreat to Black Orchard Crossing, dismount and deploy to interdict any possible water egress by a large boat from the warehouse complex." Splitting his forces made him uncomfortable, but Squad One could interdict a land escape while Squad Two could close the back door if their adversaries were planning to escape by water. "Sheffield, get us to the water, most expedient path."

Paiva felt the motion as the APC pivoted, then surged into a side street.

"Incoming," Raynald interrupted. "Targeting the cargo—"

There was a muffled *whoof* as the eighteen-wheeler behind them exploded. Pieces of wreckage clattered down on top of the APC.

"Ray, more drones, please," Paiva said drily. "We need visuals on these jokers. And send the gun truck to a good vantage point." Paiva keyed his mic. "Hawk Two, did the driver get out?"

"*Hawk Two here. The driver is with me.*"

"Excellent." Squad One now had thirteen troopers, counting the driver, plus three of his mercs. "Make your way to the complex. Secure the package, or confirm that it's gone AWOL."

"*Will do, Hawk Two out.*"

His opposition had taken out an empty cargo truck, rather than a temporarily exposed troop carrier. As he'd thought, not a full-on ambush. Just more delaying tactics on the part of someone who didn't want to kill anybody if they could avoid it.

Fortunately, he didn't have the same qualms about killing.

Sheffield piped up, "Somebody needs an ass-kicking."

Paiva bared his teeth in a predatory grin. "You got that right." Nothing like a little opposition to liven up an otherwise boring day. He was looking forward to teaching these asswipes what it meant to run up against some serious mercenaries.

Warehouse Complex (Bldg. 6), 02:24

Emily heard a distant boom at same time as she heard a lengthy crackle from her headset. That must have been the "Midnight Special" that Fang had mentioned on comms.

Looking around to find Laney, she spotted the soldier already jogging in her direction.

As Laney came to a stop next to her, Emily said, "What just happened?"

"We dropped a mini-EMP on a column of vehicles, maybe ten blocks away. Including two troop carriers and a gun truck. All told, maybe thirty-odd soldiers plus odds and sods." Laney paused. "And a team of mercs, it looks like. This shit's getting serious. We've got to be out of here in five minutes."

Suddenly, the EMP didn't seem like such overkill after all.

Emily turned and started shouting out orders. Laney pitched in to help with some of the heavy lifting, as did Emily as soon as she got things moving faster. That had to be on Fang's orders.

"Five minutes," Laney called out. "We're done."

Busy helping the others, the time had gone even faster than Emily had realized. Looking around, she quickly spotted at least a dozen boxes still left. She saw some of the other laborers come to the same conclusion as they stopped working and looked around.

Emily bowed to the inevitable. "All right everybody, let's get out of here."

"Beggin' your pardon," one of the laborers said, a Frenchman from Bordeaux. "But we're not leaving anything behind." He gestured at the remaining boxes. "This is our world's heritage."

The other workers nodded in agreement, then went back to moving boxes. Emily looked over at Laney. "Do whatever you have to. Get us another five minutes." She couldn't help it. She was proud of her workers.

She smiled humorlessly as Laney threw up her hands in aggravation. Then the soldier stood still for a moment, probably relaying the unwelcome news to Ghost One.

"Make it happen, Emily," Laney said. "It's going to be tight. I've got to join the others." She turned and ran out of the warehouse in a blur of augmented speed.

15. Fighting Retreat

Favela (Landbound), 02:30

Fang Li, Ghost One, lay prone on the roof of a decrepit two-story dwelling, stealth mode engaged, and watched Ophelia's feed as his enemies flanked him on his left side. They had what looked like a slightly over-strength squad, augmented by a small number of mercenaries with similar gear to his own.

"*You've got three mercs to deal with,*" Ophelia said. "*They weren't chameleon when they exited the troop carrier.*"

"Ghost Team," Fang said, "gloves off. Let's buy the *artistes* some more time."

They'd given their pursuers two warnings, the mini-EMP and the cargo truck. Apparently that hadn't been enough to discourage them, so the bastards had earned what was going to happen next.

Fang focused his attention on the scope view of his Samson X4 Rifle Launcher, a heavily customized Mexican weapon. He triggered a burst as one of his pursuers, a regular Brazilian trooper, emerged from cover and darted across the street.

The three explosive rounds automatically diverged in flight to bracket his target's position. The triptych of explosions shredded the soldier while Fang rolled away to avoid the inevitable backlash.

Return fire pounded the building, then an explosion took out the area where Fang had been lying. By then, though, Fang was already dropping into the alley behind the building.

"*Electrified one merc,*" Ghost Two said. The entire evolution had used Fang as bait to flush out and incapacitate at least one of the mercs stiffening up the opposing force. He'd used a "Buzz" grenade, which lit the target up with a ridiculous amount of voltage and essentially turned a combat suit into a useless piece of junk.

"*And I got two more troopers,*" added Laney.

Fang smiled grimly and jogged down the alley to the next holding position he'd selected. Rearguard actions were *so* much fun. Not.

Hawk APC, 02:33

"Hawk Three's been bricked, boss," Raynald said, looking back at Paiva, who raised an eyebrow in surprise. Paiva knew of that kind of tech, but hadn't yet managed to get his hands on any of it. It meant they'd just lost a very expensive combat suit, plus Hawk Three would probably be unconscious for a few hours or so. "Plus three of the regulars are gone. Whoever these jokers are, they're good."

Paiva gave him a grim look. "Let's get a jammer up, mess with their comms."

An icon popped into the bottom of his view field indicating that General Diego was trying to get hold of Paiva on the special communication channel Raynald had set up for him. Unsurprising, given the mini-EMP. Paiva ignored it. He was busy and he didn't need management oversight right now.

"Squad One," Paiva said, keying his mic. "Keep up the close pursuit by whatever means available." That would keep the pressure on whoever was acting as rearguard for the art thieves, and also make it harder for them to rejoin their compatriots. "Squad Two, ETA?"

"*Hawk Four, we're on station. Dismounting now.*" Good. They were now below the thieves. By heading east, they'd be in a position to interdict their escape routes.

"Spread out. Stop any boat you see. And be aware that the opposing mercs of their rearguard are top-notch; they may try escaping underwater individually." He would have, if he were in their position.

He was hopeful that he'd be able to mousetrap his enemy's fighters between his two squads. It was lucky his mercs had been embedded with the regulars—the EMP had fried all of the electronics the Brazilians had, including their supposedly hardened communication gear.

Even Squad Two's troop carrier had lost its electronics and was running at about fifty-percent fuel efficiency.

As for the thieves back at the warehouse, Paiva was almost certain they'd try to escape by water. They'd need a sizable cargo boat to carry all of the loot.

By Paiva's rough reckoning, it was going to be a close-run thing to get Squad Two, his blocking force, in place before the boat passed. It all depended on when the thieves left the warehouse, if they hadn't done so already.

Still, if they failed to block the getaway boat, they might be able to get themselves some hostages to use as leverage if they could subdue the rearguard. And Paiva had some ideas on how to catch that boat, no matter what.

He changed the comms channel and answered General Diego's call. "Paiva here." He ignored the general's ranting, then cut in when the man relented long enough to take a breath. "We've got a problem. Someone's trying to steal the package. I need choppers and more troops and I need them now."

Paiva didn't like to have his nose bloodied, and he tended to hit back a *lot* harder than he'd been hit. It was past time for some payback.

Warehouse Complex, 02:42

Laney, Ghost Three, fired her Marauder pistol, then scooted back around the corner of the warehouse to avoid the return fire, which chewed up the cinderblock and peppered her with concrete chips. Being outnumbered was not fun.

Not for the first time, she thought it might be time for a safer career. The problem, as always, was that this one paid so well, as long as you survived. She was just another export from a fractured and declining America, a well-trained but unemployed soldier with no real marketable skills except those demanded by the mercenary trade.

She heard a large explosion, undoubtedly one of Ghost Team's pursuers encountering the minefield in front of the gate. A little bit of insurance that Fang had set up when he took the gatehouse. She took the opportunity to pop off a few more shots.

Safely under cover again, she said, "Ghost Three, anybody there?" She'd hoped the relatively close proximity to her comrades would allow her signal to punch through the jamming, but no such luck. Whoever the enemy was, they were well-equipped. Definitely not a regular Batista unit.

She began moving back to the alternate zone Fang had designated right before the jamming started. The front minefield and the current firing positions of Ghost Team should subtly direct the enemy counter-clockwise around the complex to the next logical spot where they could blow the fence and get in. Right where Ghost Two had earlier set up his own minefield.

"*Ophelia here, comms are back, I took out the jammer drone.*" Laney could hear the satisfaction in the tech's voice. Couldn't ask for a better tech.

"*Ghost Three,*" Fang said, "*move to zones as planned, harry our pursuers, then exfiltrate at all possible speed.*

16. Casting Off

Warehouse Complex (Bldg. 6), 02:45

Emily pounded up the boat ramp, her arms aching from holding up her end of a pine box containing at least five or six medium-sized paintings. The Frenchman was handling the other end; he showed her a crazed grin and wild eyes as he backed up the ramp so quickly it was difficult for her to keep up. It sounded like there was a herd of buffalo on her heels as the rest of the workers rushed aboard with the last remaining boxes.

She heard the *pop-pop-pop* of gunfire somewhere behind them followed a moment later by a loud explosion. Then more gunfire.

"Get us untied!" Emily yelled, before she realized that Gregorio was already releasing the ropes holding the stern of the boat to the dock's piling.

Another man took over her load, and he and the Frenchman darted away with the box. She hurried toward the bridge as the stern started drifting away from the dock; there was a loud splash as the boarding ramp fell into the water.

Another laborer had untied the bow. Gregorio darted into the bridge right behind her. Emily settled into her seat and reached for her headset as Gregorio took the controls.

"COB here. What's the situation?"

"*The bad guys just ran into our minefield on the other side of the warehouse complex*," Ophelia said. "*They are not happy with us.*"

"I bet."

The boat's engine was already idling; now that she was still, Emily could feel the thrum of the oversized engines through the deck. The vibration combined with the butterflies in her stomach to make her queasy.

They'd gotten the paintings, but they already had armed opposition after them. Now that the possibility of danger had become the actuality, Emily was scared, both for herself and all the people on the mission. But excited, too, which rather surprised her.

Fang broke into the command channel. "*COB, don't worry about Ghost Team. We'll cover your back trail and then self-extract.*"

"COB confirms Ghost Team self-extraction." Fang clearly thought things were getting really ugly. Emily found herself in agreement with his assessment, and wasn't happy that much of it was her fault, attributable to the delays in moving all the boxes. "Ghost Team, good luck and Godspeed."

Gregorio flashed her a smile and then gunned the boat away from the dock. No need to wait for Ghost Team now.

"All the things I've smuggled in my time," he said, expertly maneuvering the boat through the gate, "and this isn't even really illegal." He shook his head.

Emily laughed. "Well, that won't keep the wrong people from shooting at us." As if to punctuate her words, she heard more sustained gunfire and another explosion in the distance.

Ophelia updated Emily on the overall situation while Gregorio maneuvered the boat at frightening speed into the narrow channels of the *favela.*

Hawk APC, 02:45

"I've got the boat," Raynald announced, putting it on the screen. It was still tied up, though it looked like the stern was swinging away from the dock. The screen suddenly went blank and Raynald started cursing.

"Trouble?" Paiva asked mildly.

"Hunter/Killer swarm," he said in an exasperated tone. "They just took out my closest eyeballs." He put a still shot of the boat back up on Paiva's screen. "I just sent this out to the squads, this is what we'll be looking for." He shook his head sadly. "You gotta get me some better toys, boss."

"*Hawk Two here. The warehouse is empty. Repeat, the warehouse is empty. We also found the guard. He was tranquilized.*" The sound of gunfire could be heard in the background.

Paiva quirked his lips up in a grim smile. "Well, at least we know who we're dealing with now." The Chinese didn't use tranquilizers and neither did the various Brazilian factions. He looked around the cramped cabin of the APC, where Raynald and Sheffield were both looking at him expectantly. "Monumentalists."

Raynald nodded. "Makes sense. If General Diego put out some feelers about selling any of the art on the international black market, their hackers could have gotten wind of it."

Sheffield glanced back at Paiva over his shoulder. "What are Monumentalists?" Ever the professional driver, he returned his attention to navigating the APC through the narrow side streets.

Paiva stared at him. Sheffield was a great driver, but not a whiz at current events.

Raynald saved him the trouble of answering. "They recover priceless artwork stolen during the world's conflicts. Been around in one form or another for a couple centuries." He grimaced. "Basically, a bunch of well-funded do-gooders who are about to steal our mission bonuses from us."

Sheffield growled, "Not on my watch."

The APC lurched as Sheffield braked sharply. Paiva looked up at the main screen and saw that they'd come to a stop about twenty meters from some ramshackle housing. The street was a dead end, and too narrow to turn around in easily.

"The water's on the other side of that shack," Sheffield said apologetically. I need to find another route."

"No time," Paiva responded. "Go through it." Sheffield looked at him with wide eyes. "APC vs. shack—the APC wins every time."

The driver shrugged. He revved the engine and smashed through the building, broken boards and debris flying everywhere. The front end of the APC splashed down into the water and momentum carried them beyond the wreckage of the dwelling. Paiva couldn't tell if anybody had been in the building, or not. He didn't much care, either. You got used to collateral damage after a while.

The APC floated, just as it was designed to do. There was a rumble as Sheffield withdrew the wheels into their compartments. As soon as the transformation to boat mode was complete, Sheffield hit the throttle and the APC took off in pursuit of the Monumentalists.

It wasn't the fastest boat around, but Paiva figured it was probably faster than the cargo boat they were chasing. The Russians built a good product.

RECOVERY OP

The Veteran in a New Field, by Winslow Homer, 1865. Oil on canvas. OWU Catalog #198.

Painted soon after Confederate General Robert E. Lee's surrender and President Abraham Lincoln's assassination, the painting depicts a Union veteran, as evidenced by the discarded jacket and canteen at lower right, who is now tackling a field of wheat instead of the field of battle.

The old-fashioned scythe evokes the Grim Reaper, symbolizing the Civil War's grim harvest of death. The painting is somehow rendered even more poignant with the knowledge that the Union did not last. The United States of America broke into five nations at the culmination of Civil War II.

17. A New Plan

Warehouse Complex, Near Back Gate, 02:49

Bullets tunneled through the water past Laney, slowing rapidly due to the resistance, as the DPV pulled her into the depths of the man-made lagoon around the warehouse complex. One of her pursuers, probably the merc, had been using explosive flechette rounds. She was dazed and her head was still ringing from the buffeting she'd taken from the explosive impacts, but at least she hadn't let go of the DPV. Luckily, her suit was only slightly damaged, at least according to her bleary view of her heads-up display.

She heard a hiss and accompanying sting as the suit injected her with something to help her cope with the situation. The fog clouding her thought processes began to clear, enough for her to realize she was in deep trouble. Got to love those combat drugs. You might die, but at least your mind will be clear.

Ophelia's voice penetrated her rapidly evaporating semi-stupor. "*Ghost Three! Get out of there! Enemy APC incoming!*"

She dove for cover on the debris-covered bottom, then she felt pain, a lot of pain, as everything around her exploded and the world went black.

Hawk APC, 02:50

"Got one!" Raynald exulted, throwing his hands up in the air.

One of the screens showed the view of the lagoon behind them; water was still falling from the missile strike.

Paiva smiled grimly. In his experience, there was no such thing as overkill.

Squad One could pursue the other two mercs from the enemy's rearguard. His quarry was the boat. And they couldn't be more than a few minutes behind it.

Cargo Boat, 02:53

"*Ghost Three is flatline.*"

Emily hung her head, tears in her eyes. She was in command of the mission. Ghost Three was a casualty, her first. And it was her fault. God, she'd liked Laney, and now she was dead.

Gregorio looked over at her with concern, understanding that something bad had just happened. "What's wrong?"

"Laney's dead."

He crossed his heart. "It's like smuggling," he said gently. "Which I've done a lot of in my time." He paused to swing the boat through a tight turn. "You accept the risks when you take the job. We all did."

"Yeah, but—"

"Now your job is to see us through this," he said firmly. "You light a candle for Laney later."

She looked at him, seeing iron where before she'd seen just an uneducated local. Suddenly she could envision Gregorio as the patriarch doing whatever it took to keep his extended family safe through decades of vicious warfare.

She nodded, then keyed the mic. "How are we looking?"

"*Not good,*" Ophelia said. "*The enemy APC functions as a boat, and they're catching up. We're inbound to help out, but they'll intercept first.*"

"Understood," Emily said, studying the overhead view on her screen. "Ghost Team, I'm sorry about Laney. Now, I need you to intercept and slow down the enemy APC, or the mission's a bust." She wiped her eyes. "Unless Fang has a better idea."

"*COB, orders confirmed.*" Fang said. "*Concur with your assessment.*"

She doubted the two remaining Ghost Team fighters had the firepower to stop the APC. She'd probably just sent them to die, too.

Emily glanced over at Gregorio, who was giving her a questioning glance. He'd only heard her end of the conversation.

"Our pursuers are catching up too quickly?" he asked.

"Yes," Emily said. "They have an APC that floats like a boat, so they're not far behind us. *Paladin's* coming in, but it's slow..." She could picture *Paladin* rolling through the bottom muck of the favela, a muddy cloud in its wake.

Gregorio said, "When I was smuggling, sometimes we'd use two boats, a prime and a backup. If we were being chased, we'd do a drop and switch. You make a slight detour, if your pursuers aren't too close. Drop the cargo, then get back on your main route and lead your pursuers away. The backup boat would come in after everybody'd passed, maybe an innocent looking fishing boat or something, pick up the cargo and leisurely leave the area."

Emily tilted her head and considered him. "That...might work. I can see some problems, but..." She keyed the mic. "Ophelia, Fang, we might have a strategy. Let me run something past you."

Favela, 02:56

Fang, Ghost One, pounded down a crowded walkway, dodging around people when he could, but shoving them out of the way when he couldn't. Thanks to the fighting lots of people had been awakened and had come outside to see what was going on. At this speed, stealth made him a discernible blur rather than hiding him outright.

"Need some ideas on their APC," Fang said.

"*It's functioning as a boat, right?*" Trav asked. Ghost Two was running also, but parallel to Fang on another thoroughfare, if you could call these rickety walkways thoroughfares.

"*Yes,*" Ophelia said.

Fang passed a cantina with a roof that extended over the walkway. He grabbed a support pole and used it to round a corner without slowing down. "It's got to have weaknesses we can exploit."

"*Jane's says the Russians make an APC that floats,*" Ophelia said. "*Narrow double keel, it's part of the armor, so you'll have trouble damaging that. It's got a rudder, but that looks hard to damage, too. It's water-propelled. Like a jet engine, sucking water in the front using some turbo-props and then jetting it out the back.*"

"So," Fang said, "we take out the jet and it's dead in the water?"

"*Um, two jets, actually. And filters to keep gunk away from the turboprop.*"

"*I sense a plan here,*" Trav said.

"What about witnesses to the drop-off?" Fang asked.

"*My problem,*" Emily said. "*We'll handle it.*"

For a plan cobbled together on the fly, it wasn't terrible. Except, of course, for the part where he and Ghost Two had to take on an APC.

"Execute," Fang said, checking the overhead drone view on his heads-up.

In a moment, he'd worked out the ambush location and timing with Ophelia. The enemy APC was coming up behind him, still out of sight because of the twists and turns of the waterway. Ghost Two smashed his way through somebody's house and emerged on the walkway on the opposite side of the waterway from him.

At almost the same moment, they both leaped feet-first into the water and looked for sheltered positions amongst the pilings that supported the buildings. The water was about fifteen feet deep.

Clinging to a slick, moss-covered piling, Fang reached over his shoulder and pulled the minelayer, a twin to the one that Ghost Two had used earlier, off his back. One hundred pellet mines in an operator-selectable spray pattern. Ghost Two still had half of his load left; the half he'd deployed previously had cost the enemy another of their hi-tech mercs.

So they had a total of one hundred and fifty pellets to put in the path of the APC. Surely, at least some of those would be sucked into the APC's jet intakes.

Fang keyed in some parameters for the pattern and operation of the mines.

"Go deep, Trav," Fang said. It was probably the only chance either one of them had to survive this.

18. Ambush

Hawk APC, 02:58

On the screen, Paiva observed the enemy boat barreling through the waterways just two blocks ahead of them. It wouldn't be long now.

"Not again," Raynald said, exasperated, as the overhead drone view disappeared from the screen. "They've got some HK's left, too." Hunter-Killer drones, for taking out other drones. Raynald turned toward him. "Boss, we gotta get—"

The warning alarm went off. Paiva heard the sound of metallic impacts against the lower hull.

Raynald said, "Oh shit, we're being attacked," which was something Paiva had already figured out.

Then the APC was engulfed in an explosion that made the hull ring and slammed Paiva against the bulkhead. The nose of the APC surged upward and the whole craft corkscrewed left. There was a crash as the vehicle slammed into the pilings of the buildings that lined the waterway. Then more crashes and heavy thumps, as wreckage fell on them.

Paiva looked over at his tech, safely belted into his seat but still dazed from the explosive concussion. Paiva activated the APC's antipersonnel weaponry himself, which was still mostly operational. Around the circumference of the APC, barrels popped out of their slots. High-speed explosive rounds exploded against every obstacle in the vicinity of the APC, with each round spewing titanium flechettes in a deadly circle.

The effect was if someone had taken a buzz-saw and chopped out the wooden supports for every building within one hundred and fifty meters of the APC. As one, the already rickety structures collapsed into the water, taking an unknown number of people into the water with them.

Depressing the barrels as low as they'd go, Paiva next turned the water immediately around the APC into a churning froth.

The weapons finally silent, Paiva looked over at Sheffield, his driver. "Damage report?"

Sheffield cleared his throat, uncomfortable at giving him bad news. "They took out one of our jets and damaged the other. We've got about seventy-five percent power on the one jet, but we can only use about fifty if we want to go straight. Figure quarter speed, boss."

"Raynald?"

"Attacks from both sides," he answered. "I figure you just took care of both remaining mercs. Meanwhile, they took out two more drones while we were busy."

Cargo Boat, 03:01

As soon as Ophelia announced that it was safe, Gregorio took the boat into a narrow side waterway. While the boat slowed down, Emily ran out onto the deck and made her way to the cramped cabin behind the bridge where the rest of the crew was waiting.

"We're dropping the cargo pod right here, right now," Emily said, as her team gaped at her in surprise.

"What about the plan?" Sanford sputtered.

"This is the new plan, the old one went out the window. *Paladin* is on its way and is going to pick us all up, but we've got to get this done during a narrow window, so move!"

Emily flattened herself against the cabin wall as the men sprang into action, all except Sanford and the other art historian, a Swedish woman.

Remaining seated, Sanford raised his eyebrows and took a puff of his pipe. "I hope you know what you're doing?"

Emily said, "Makin' it up as I go along. I hope the cargo pod's watertight, though."

Sanford laughed. "Me, too."

Emily went back out on deck. The boat was just drifting slowly now. There were people on both sides of the waterway, perhaps twenty in all, watching their activities with curiosity.

Gregorio sauntered out of the bridge, grabbed a handhold and clambered onto the roof of the boat.

Standing, legs spread apart and somehow looking like a force of nature, he began speaking to the crowd in Portuguese. Emily had no idea what he was saying, but she clicked her mic both so that Ophelia could hear and so that it could be recorded for later review.

When she reached the back of the boat, the crew had the fake door open, exposing the wide cargo pod that occupied the back two-thirds of the boat's deckhouse. As she watched, it slid out on its rails, a metal box painted in jungle camouflage colors. It smashed the wooden railings and rolled off the end of the boat, dropping into the water with a mighty splash.

It disappeared into the muddy water as if it had never been. Billions of creds of irreplaceable artwork, just dropped into the polluted water to land in the mud. If this didn't work out, not only would she likely end up dead, but she'd go down in history as the biggest destroyer of artwork since the Nazis in the twentieth century. She wasn't sure which she dreaded more.

As Emily walked back toward the bow, Gregorio climbed down from the roof. A moment later, he'd nudged the boat over to the nearest walkway, which came to about two feet above the boat's railing.

Between her own laborers and eager volunteers from above, they brought the boat to a stop against the walkway.

"Everybody off," Emily shouted. "Let's go!"

Under Hawk APC, 03:06

Fang sprawled in the muck about ten feet under the keel of the enemy APC in a pocket of water undisturbed by the maelstrom of weapons fire from the vehicle above. He had no idea what had happened to Trav or the entire neighborhood around them, but it was undoubtedly bad. In the meantime, he'd turned all his emissions off and was trying to look, as much as possible, like debris simply half embedded in the mud. There was certainly enough real wreckage drifting down around him to augment his subterfuge.

Hawk APC, 03:09

"Get us out of here," Paiva snarled.

The APC shuddered as Sheffield complied by levering the craft back and forth to loosen the wreckage that had fallen on it. There was a sharp jerk as the damaged vehicle finally pulled free, only to immediately bump into more debris floating in the waterway.

While Sheffield navigated the debris field they'd created, Paiva looked over Raynald's shoulder for a sitrep. The escaping boat was visible on one of the screens powering down a main channel, but the view was jerky. An overlay showed the boat's distance from them, about a klick away and moving faster than they could with the damage they'd been dealt.

Pointing at the jerky view, "Is that one of Diego's choppers?"

"Yeah," Raynald said. "Just got here. The HK's won't be taking that out." HK's were good against eyeballs, but not larger targets. They just didn't have the size for significant firepower.

"So they can stop the boat?"

"Yeah, but I don't trust their accuracy, boss." Raynald gave him an evil grin. "I have a better idea."

19. Scattered Forces

In or Around *La Bomba*, 03:10

Despite being surrounded by her *artistes*, Emily had never felt as alone as she did when the boat disappeared around the corner. She was stranded in the middle of a war zone, with both international mercenaries and Brazilian soldiers actively hunting them. And no pickup anywhere in sight.

She turned and considered Miller, leaning on the weathered railing beside her looking down at the diminishing waves from the departing boat's wake. "We can't stay outside like this," Emily said, "we stick out like a sore thumb."

Miller nodded. "OK, let me see what I can do."

On the journey upriver, she'd compiled a skills matrix for everybody on the mission, including, as much as they'd answer questions, Ghost Team. Miller's first wife—he was now on his fifth, making him a dedicated serial monogamist—had been a Brazilian refugee. He still spoke passable Portuguese.

He spoke to a few of the onlookers, who pointed further down the walkway. "This way," he called out.

The *artistes* followed him, Sanford and another man each carrying bulky, square paintings that hadn't fit within the now submerged container. Another carried a rolled up painting wrapped in canvas with strings around it, which made Emily cringe a little bit. Hell of a way to carry a priceless painting around.

Miller disappeared into a dark doorway ahead of them, then came out a few seconds later. Smiling, he said, "Local bomb shelter. We have to go in one at a time."

He stood by the door conversing amiably with several of the locals while they took turns going through the door. She studied the building. Just a slap-dash, wooden building on stilts, like everything else in the *favela.* Didn't look safer than the other buildings, despite the words "Bomb Shelter" written in neat block letters above the doorway, beneath a phrase in larger lettering that presumably had once said the same thing in Portuguese. Someone had crudely spray painted "LA BOMBA" over the text.

Miller held the door open for her, then closed it after her when she entered. She found herself in almost total darkness, within what seemed to be a closet-sized foyer. Then she realized there was some yellow light leaking around the irregular edges of the wall in front of her. Reaching out, she touched cloth and realized there was a black curtain in front of her. Pushing through, she found herself standing next to Sanford in what was clearly a bar.

As drinking establishments went, it was a dive. The tables were long planks laid across upright barrels. The bar was a bunch of large wooden boxes arranged in an L-shape. The shelves behind the bar held bottles, most of which didn't have labels, and ceramic jars. None of the chairs and stools in front of the bar matched. And most of the customers at the tables were sitting on what looked like wooden produce crates. The windows were shuttered; the bar was clearly operating in blackout mode, as if that made a difference with modern weapons.

There were plenty of people, of diverse ages, and most of them were looking at her group with unfeigned curiosity.

She moved to the side as Miller came through behind her. He was followed immediately by several of the locals that Miller had been talking to, who started circulating amongst the crowd and gesticulating dramatically.

Miller said, "The Chinese have been bombing nightly, but they pretty much leave the *favela* alone."

"Makes sense," Emily said. "It'd be a waste of ordinance."

"Yeah, well, it makes it hard to sleep. So of lot of these folks'll hang out drinking at night, and work or sleep during the day."

Emily raised her voice, so the group could hear her, and said, "We need to scatter and blend in. Everybody grab a seat somewhere. Make sure you're surrounded by Brazilians. And get the paintings and the guns out of sight."

They looked at her blankly for a moment. Exasperated, she said, "Go!" The *artistes* scattered.

Once the crowd figured out what they were trying to do, they went out of their way to help. The way Emily figured it, by this point in the war, the locals hated the Batistas and the Chinese-led coalition about equally. None of them needed to be geniuses to realize that neither side cared about them.

Emily walked up to the bar and dropped a few small gold coins on the bar. The bartender, a bald old man with a five-day beard and a paunch, grinned ebulliently and made them disappear.

Drinks were pushed into all of their hands. Miller ended up with a woman sitting in his lap while Sanford ended up sitting with a mob of young men, his painting safely hidden underneath the table. A group of twenty-somethings surrounded Emily at the bar. One of them, strikingly handsome and severely aware of it, casually put his arm around her waist as if she were his girlfriend.

Ambush Site (Underwater), 03:12

As soon as the APC's propeller noise disappeared into the distance, Fang extracted himself from the bottom muck and went looking for Travis. Visibility was effectively zero, so he trudged along the bottom in total darkness—the combat suit and his remaining gear made him somewhat less than buoyant—guided electronically toward Trav's last location.

"Trav?" No answer from Ghost Two. Not good. "Ophelia?"

He wasn't too surprised when Ophelia didn't answer. With the enemy approaching, she'd probably brought the drone that had been relaying their communications down amongst the buildings to avoid detection and elimination. Incongruously, that had probably made it a casualty of their opposition's response to being ambushed. He was incommunicado until she got another drone on station.

Fang hated to admit it, but whoever their adversaries were, they were good.

And ruthless as well. They clearly couldn't care less about collateral damage.

He reached Ghost Two's location and found a mass of shattered pilings and shredded wooden debris; the remains of the building above had been dropped on Ghost Two's position.

"Trav?"

This time he thought he heard some static, so he climbed around the pile to see if he could get a better signal. The debris shifted and he had to jump to avoid getting his leg trapped between two thick beams. He figured he was getting close to Trav when he started hearing cursing interspersed with the static.

"Ghost Two, state your status."

The cursing stopped. "*Blown up, sir.*"

Inside his helmet, Fang rolled his eyes. Ghost Two couldn't be too badly hurt, not if he still had his sense of humor intact.

They were close enough now that his combat suit was able to handshake with Ghost Two's suit, giving Fang access to Trav's diagnostics. His suit was pretty banged up. The left arm was usable but unpowered. The right leg had been breached, and Trav was bleeding, but not badly; internal seals were keeping water out of the rest of his suit. His longer distance comms had been scraped off, leaving him with perhaps a twenty-meter communications range. His rifle was damaged and unusable, though he still had his pistol.

"Time for you to stop lying around and get back to work, trooper."

"*OK, but can you get this building off me?*" Ghost Two said. "*I'm trapped under a couple of big beams and I don't have the leverage to move them.*"

The AI in Fang's combat suit helpfully highlighted Ghost Two's precise position. He started pulling debris out of the way.

Ophelia said, "*Ghost One, Ghost Two, check, check.*"

Without stopping his efforts, and breathing heavily with exertion despite the powered assist from the suit, Fang answered, "Ghost One here. Ghost Two is slightly dented, but fine. He's got a comms problem, but my suit can relay for him as long as we're within about twenty meters of each other."

20. DISTRACTION

Cargo Boat, 03:16

Gregorio braced himself as he piloted the boat through a sweeping turn that took it from the main channel through the watery *favela* and into a side channel. The back end swung a little wide and smashed against one of the timbers holding up a walkway. He ignored the damage to the boat; he was planning to abandon the boat as soon as he got past one more turn.

He missed having Emily's connection with Ghost Team—it sure was nice to have their bird's eye view of the area. But he felt he wasn't doing too badly. His years of smuggling experience had given him a feel for the rhythm of this kind of chase.

He hoped he'd muddied his backtrail enough that the enemy couldn't figure out where he'd dropped his passengers, not even when they found this boat abandoned. Two more minutes and he'd step off this boat for the last time and just fade into the local population.

His employers had already gotten his family out of Brazil. He'd hide out for a couple weeks, and then take advantage of the same contacts his family had been given to get out himself. Just a few weeks and he'd be able to see his grandchildren again.

Four kilometers away, Paiva's gun truck pulled to a halt on a street that provided an elevated view of the *favela.* It was a nice neighborhood, save for a few homes that had been demolished by bombing. The gun swiveled in response to precise, real-time coordinates provided by Raynald's helicopter view and fired a single shot from its mass driver.

At almost fifteen thousand kilometers per hour, the supersonic crash of the shot broke windows throughout the neighborhood. The metallic projectile flashed into a cyan plasma that looked more like a laser bolt than a high-speed projectile. It tunneled through one of the neighborhood homes, obliterating the living room and the family dog. It cut a groove through the roof of a building in the *favela.*

The bolt passed through a crowded tenement, missing a man by seven meters who had just gotten out of bed, but sucking him out of the wide exit hole and depositing him in the water with just a few broken bones and minor burns. It evaporated a couple making love in their tiny but neat home, then smashed through the cabin of the boat.

The shot missed Gregorio by two meters but it didn't matter. At that proximity, his body was disintegrated, sucked out the exit hole and spread over an area of about a hundred meters as a fine red mist. The cabin effectively ceased to exist. The impact drove the boat into the far side of the channel where it crashed into a building, which partially collapsed onto the bow of the boat.

***Paladin*, 03:17**

"Jesus," Ophelia said, wide-eyed. "They just took out the boat."

"What?" Armel exclaimed, without turning around. "How?" He kept his eyes on the screens in front of him.

Navigating *Paladin* underwater through the *favela* had never been part of the plan. It was an improvisation born of necessity. Unlike the opposition's APC, *Paladin* didn't float. It rolled across the bottom on its tracks, like an old-fashioned tank, but more agile. Ophelia knew it was taking all of Armel's attention and skills to make sure they didn't get stuck in the mud, hung up on the junk that littered the bottom, or smash into obstacles, like the pilings that supported the buildings around them; that would give their presence away.

Keying her mic, Ophelia said, "Ghost Team, the boat has been stopped. Rail gun. Looks like it was the gun truck we saw earlier. While we've been busy, they moved it to an elevated position and blasted us."

"Shit," Armel said. "I prefer my bad guys to be incompetent."

"Me, too," Ophelia said, fervently.

"*Shoulda taken that out when we had the chance,*" Travis drawled. "*I guess we're gonna need to keep our heads down.*"

"*Ghost One, ETA on* Paladin*?*"

"Five minutes," Armel said, chiming in on comms, "but we're going to need your help to get the container attached."

Ophelia cursed. She'd been so worried about coordinating things that she'd forgotten about that. Their testing back on *Khufu* had demonstrated that enhanced strength was needed to make the attachment under field conditions. Plus neither she nor Armel had any underwater gear.

"*Ghost One here, we're on our way.*"

"*Yeah, dented but still in service. Mostly.*"

Favela (Underwater), 03:23

Fang bounded over some twisted pilings, moving through the murky water as if he were in a slow motion movie scene. He and Trav had made their way along the bottom across the wreckage of the surrounding buildings. The combat suits were relatively light, thanks to various composite materials, but only relatively. They still floated like bricks. Swimming wasn't an option, even with the strength augmentation.

"*Ah, the scenic tour,*" Trav said. "*You take me to all the good places, Fang.*"

Fang ignored his chatter, knowing that it was just how Trav kept his spirits up in the thick of the action, and focused on the task at hand. A lot of ramshackle wooden buildings had been dropped into the water when the pilings had been chewed out from underneath them. Those closest to the ambush had been further pulverized by the anti-personnel rounds from the enemy APC. This far from the epicenter, the wreckage was looking considerably less chewed up.

Ophelia said, "*Paladin is on station. Ghost One, Ghost Two, we're waiting on you guys now.*"

Up ahead, Fang spotted some pilings emerging from the murk that had been damaged but not destroyed. They'd finally reached the edge of the damage zone.

"Ghost One here, we're moving. Should be out of the water momentarily."

Time to find a place to climb up.

They'd make better time on the walkways.

21. Fateful Intervention

Favela, 03:25

Hawk Four, the leader of Squad Two, jogged down the walkway, shouldering aside any locals who got in his way. Another mercenary pounded along behind him. Seven Batista soldiers were strung out in their wake, having trouble keeping up with the mercenaries, who were more fit in general and also physically augmented by their combat suits.

"*The boat's been stopped,*" Raynald said. A map appeared on his heads-up display, with the route clearly marked. Raynald was nothing if not efficient. "*Hawk Four, expedite approach before the local scavengers start stealing—*"

A bright light blossomed in the sky above, momentarily turning night into day and cutting off the signal with a crackle. Vision filters compensated for the brightness but couldn't do much about the thunderclap of the aerial explosion, which rolled over the city with near-deafening intensity.

His ears were still ringing as his companion pulled up alongside him and shouted, "That's new!" The Chinese had been bombing Manaus sporadically for the last two weeks, but not like this.

"EMP," Hawk Four responded. The full-scale strategic kind, not like the mini-EMP their opponents had used earlier. It meant that the Chinese forces would probably be making their final push against Manaus soon.

As the flare of the EMP gradually faded, missiles streaked across the sky. It looked like they were heading for downtown. Anti-missile units opened up, sending distant sparks arcing into the sky. Fiery puffballs appeared in the heavens with staccato pops. Distant explosions, probably missile and bomb strikes, added their rumble to the noise.

He saw a helicopter auto-rotating as it fell from the sky. It disappeared from view behind a building, then an expanding fireball outlined the building in billowing waves of yellow and red.

"We've still got a mission," he shouted. "Secure the boat!"

He sped up, legs blurring with augmented speed. His fellow Hawk matched his lead and they left the unaugmented soldiers in their wake.

La Bomba, 03:26

Despite the shutters on the bar's windows, light suddenly washed in around the edges, startling Emily and the rest of the bar's denizens. It had to have been momentarily brighter than day outside. The light was accompanied by a thunderclap of epic proportions.

Emily heard a crackle in her ear as her headset went dead and—wait—was it actually warmer than it had been a second ago? And something was wrong with her vision. No, not her vision. Her implants. At the bottom of her view field, she usually had the time and her geographical position displayed. Those were gone.

She looked around the bar. Sanford was on the floor, screaming in pain. He had extensive implants, a whole memory augmentation model, if she recalled correctly. A few of the others were shaking their heads, probably discovering the same thing she'd just found with her own implants.

"Had to be an EMP," Emily said as Miller came up to her.

"Yeah."

"Must be the Chinese."

The Brazilians seemed unaffected; she doubted that any of them had implants. Modern conveniences had fled Brazil long ago.

Favela, 03:30

Hawk Four pounded down the walkway at extreme speed, dodging around doglegs in his path, followed closely by Hawk Five. The walkway turned the corner at an intersection. He crashed through the railing and leaped seven meters across the canal, landing heavily on the opposite walkway. A few boards cracked as he landed but momentum carried him safely past the damage.

He didn't bother to look back as Hawk Five made the same leap behind him. He sprinted another two hundred meters then turned down a narrower side canal. According to his map, the boat was within five hundred meters, though he couldn't see it yet, due to the twists and turns of the waterway.

A few minutes later, he said, "I see it." The two mercenaries had local comms, good for about twenty meters, but the longer distance comms had fried. He subvocalized a command and a zoom window opened up on one side of his helmet view. "Looks like there's people on board."

Behind him, Hawk Five asked, "*Survivors or indigents?*"

"Tell you in a minute."

Somebody saw the mercenaries coming and people started to scatter, heading for the nearest walkway or simply jumping into the water. By then, it was too late. The two mercenaries jumped and landed side-by-side on the stern of the boat, facing the doublewide doors where the stolen paintings had presumably been stored. A stray thought stuck Hawk Four as he landed—it was odd that the back railing was broken when it was the bow that had taken the brunt of the crash. He moved left while his companion went right. Careful not to aim any shots at what they assumed was the boat's cargo compartment, they blasted away with flechette rounds that shredded anybody in sight.

Hawk Four said. “I think they were indigents, but it’s hard to tell.”

While his companion went left to check the forward section of the boat, Hawk Four walked aft to check the cargo compartment. Throwing open the unlocked doors revealed only empty space beyond.

“I think we got a problem.”

22. Tribulations

Paladin / La Bomba, 03:35

"Dammit!" Ophelia exclaimed. "I just lost everything to the EMP." Her eyeballs, and even the larger HKs that had previously taken out the enemy's jammer—all gone.

"Awesome," Armel said, shaking his head. "This situation just gets more fun by the minute."

"I'm popping our own jammer," Ophelia said, hands moving rapidly across her screens. "Zeds are spread out, their comms'll be rebooting 'cause of the EMP…let's mess with them some more." There was a popping sound and the jammer was away.

Armel chuckled. "Aren't you glad we included reimbursement for expendables in our contract?"

"Yeah." Ophelia chuckled humorlessly. "Well, we're here, and I can't tell anyone." There was no way Emily's comms survived the EMP. She turned to look at Armel. "Get us close to the walkway and deploy the access tube. I'm going to have to go up and get the *artistes*."

"But—"

"It can't be you," she said. "You have to drive. So, tag, I'm it." She unbuckled her harness.

"All right," he said dubiously, "I hope you know what you're doing." He maneuvered the APC a little closer to the walkway. Then there was a *whooshing* sound from above them as he deployed the ETR.

Ophelia stood up and undogged the hatch in the low ceiling of the vehicle, revealing the ribbed plastic tube with its built-in ladder. A few trickles of water splashed down to the deck. She grunted as she grabbed the first rung of the ladder and laboriously pulled herself up into the tube.

A moment later she was at the surface, holding on to what looked like the inner tube of a truck tire. Fortunately, Armel had positioned her right next to one of the supports for the walkway. She reached out, grabbed a weathered cross-strut, pulled herself out of the tube and clambered up to the walkway.

A few natives looked at her curiously. "Seen any foreigners?" she asked, not really expecting an answer.

An old woman with gray hair said, "In *La Bomba*," and pointed to a doorway about thirty meters away. Ophelia gave her a second look, and realized that the gray was misleading; she was probably in her late thirties.

She jogged down the walkway, pushed through the door and curtain beyond and found herself in a rundown bar. The *artistes* were present, though one of them was lying on the floor, surrounded by Emily, Miller and several others.

"We've got to get moving," Ophelia shouted. "Your ride's here and we can't stay long!"

Emily looked up, startled. She nodded and started giving directions. Two of her team members picked up the supine member of her crew; he must have been a casualty of the EMP, distinctly possible for anyone who had extensive implants.

Ophelia ushered the two carrying their casualty to the door. Three more folks followed them, each carrying a painting, with Emily bringing up the rear and herding people along.

Hawk APC, 03:36

To his left, Raynald started cursing. Paiva looked over at him. "No luck on the drones?" They were going through drones like firecrackers on Cinco de Mayo, first losing a set to the Monumentalists' mini-EMP, then a jammer and some drones to their H/K swarm, and now another set, plus their helicopter support, to the Chinese EMP. Paiva hated being out of contact with his forces, especially since he had two squads spread out trying to intercept the Monumentalists.

"Three problems," Raynald said. "First, we ain't got a gun truck no more, the Chinese killed it. Second, the Monumentalists are jamming us. Finally, the drone launch tube is damaged. I can't release anything."

Paiva sighed heavily. He was becoming decidedly weary of these damned Monumentalists. He had two squads out looking for his foes, and now he couldn't even contact them. "Anything else?" Raynald shook his head. "Can you launch the drones manually?"

"I'll need to pull the whole unit," Raynald said, "But I've got to do it from outside. I've got the tools, but it'll take a while. And I can't do it while..." Trailing off, he pointed at the screen in front of Sheffield, the APC driver.

Paiva watched impatiently as Sheffield attempted to navigate through the debris field. The engine rotors whined angrily as his driver tried to push some timbers out of their path, to no avail, as the APC-turned–boat twisted sideways rather than making forward progress.

Paiva rubbed his forehead, a telltale sign of his frustration. Sheffield was making progress, albeit painstakingly, just not fast enough for his needs. The fundamental problem was that a watercraft, any watercraft, just didn't have the leverage to force its way through the floating wreckage that surrounded them.

"I'm dismounting," Paiva snarled, unhitching the three-point harness holding him in his seat.

Sheffield looked over his shoulder. "Sorry, boss—"

"Not your fault," Paiva said, picking up his helmet. "My orders, my fault. Just get out of this mess as fast as you can." He pulled his helmet on.

"At least we pasted those Monumentalists," Sheffield said.

Paiva nodded curtly, stood up and undogged the hatch on the APC's ceiling, which popped open with a hydraulic hiss. Ignoring the pull-down ladder, he leaped up, grabbed the rim of the hatch and propelled himself to a standing position on the APC's hull.

He grimly considered the bobbing, shifting quagmire of floating timbers, demolished housing, furniture and bodies that surrounded the APC. Ignoring the collateral damage, to which he was largely inured to by now in his lengthy military career, he simply considered the unstable terrain as an obstacle to be crossed. Choosing a large piece that looked relatively stable, he leapt onto it and began making his way through the wreckage.

Outside La Bomba, 03:39

Emily helped one of her people lift Sanford over the railing, gently passing him to someone else down below, who then slid him into the arms of Miller waiting in the opening of the tube. Ophelia and two other team members stood behind Emily, guarding the extra paintings and watching the struggle to get Sanford down to the *Paladin.*

"Uh, Emily," Ophelia said, "we've got a problem."

Emily turned around and saw a combat-suited mercenary behind them, holding a massive rifle pointed at Ophelia. As she watched, a group of perhaps six Brazilian soldiers filtered down the walkway toward them, guns also aimed in this direction.

"We were so close," Emily said.

"Why don't you ask your guys to climb back up over the railing?" the mercenary said. "Or we can shoot them. Your call."

"All right," Emily said. "You win." Keeping her hands clearly in view, she turned slightly and called out, "Come on back up, you guys."

One man, the one who'd been passing Sanford down to Miller, climbed slowly back over the railing. There was a burst of gunfire behind him as several of the soldiers fired on Miller and Sanford. Emily leaned forward and saw the tube floating below, Miller well down in the accessway and still holding Sanford in front of him. She didn't see any signs of blood. As she watched, they fell into the APC. She couldn't tell for sure, but somebody may have slammed the hatch behind them.

Emily faced the mercenary. It was disconcerting seeing her face reflected in the shiny surface of the mercenary's helmet. And even more upsetting to see a very large gun pointed directly at her.

"This is Hawk Two," the mercenary said. "Can anyone read me? Squad One has captured the thieves." Apparently, he wasn't having luck getting hold of anyone. Hawk Two gestured at Emily with his weapon. "What do you have down there in the water?"

"A mini-sub," Emily said, figuring that the best lie was the one that contained at least enough truth to be plausible.

"Makes sense," he said. "Tell them to surface now, or we'll start shooting some of your people."

"They won't listen," Emily said. "If you were them and you had the perfect getaway vehicle, would you surface?"

Emily tried not to react as Fang appeared on the roof above Hawk Two. He fired a stubby-looking gun with a large barrel at the enemy mercenary. It hit the mercenary and enveloped his suit in something that looked like an electrical storm. Emily dived away from Hawk Two, then felt her arm get singed by an electrical discharge as she reached out to sweep a rolled-up painting out of the way. The mercenary fell heavily, clearly out of commission, whether unconscious or dead, Emily couldn't tell.

"Down!" she yelled as the soldiers fired back at Fang. Ophelia was already down, but her *artistes* hit the deck as well, huddling with fear and trying not to appear like viable targets. Some of the soldiers fell, thanks to Fang's intense return barrage. Then Travis appeared behind the soldiers and caught them in a crossfire.

Half deaf from all the gunfire, Emily had time to realize that the gun battle had only lasted perhaps thirty seconds. All of the combatants except Fang and Travis were down. Where the soldiers had been, blood and body parts were splattered everywhere.

Fang jumped down from the roof, landing next to Emily with a solid thud. "Let's get everybody loaded," he said. "It's time to get the hell out of here."

Ophelia said, "We need one of you guys to hook up the container."

Walking up, Travis said, "It's going to have to be you, Fang. My suit's too damaged." Emily tried hard not to stare. His formerly shiny and pristine combat suit was so dented and scraped up it looked like somebody had run it through a washing machine.

"All right," Fang said. The whole walkway shook as he jumped over the railing and into the water.

23. Action

Favela, 03:42

Paiva was angry. Not only was he out of position, admittedly due to his own perhaps overly enthusiastic suppression fire, but now he was completely cut off from his squads, too. He'd expected comms back by now, but the Monumentalists were still jamming.

Hearing gunfire in the distance, he sped up even more.

Somebody was going to very sorry when he arrived.

Favela, 03:45

Fang stood in the mud and glumly contemplated the dilemma before him. The problem was twofold. First, the container and *Paladin* were at slightly different levels. Second, Fang had no leverage; he kept sinking into the mud every time he tried to exert enough force to get the container hitched up.

What he really need was a winch to raise the container a bit. Well, he had rope with him, in a compartment. Actually a cable. Standard military gear.

"Armel," Fang said. "I want you to swivel the main gun so it's over the container. I'm going to improvise a winch."

"*Ghost One, I could use one of those, too,*" Travis drawled, "*but I typically wait until after the mission.*"

Outside La Bomba, 03:46

Emily watched as her last team member, a Swedish woman in her mid-forties, climbed down to the floating tube. Clinging to the pylon, the woman reached out with a foot, hooked the inner tube and pulled it closer. Then she gingerly climbed into the tube. She stopped partway and reached up as Emily hung off the railing and handed the last painting to her, the one that had been rolled up for safekeeping.

Emily straightened up and looked around. It was just her and Travis now, and Fang down in the water working on the connector. Unexpectedly, she was looking in the right direction as two more combat-suited mercenaries raced around a corner.

"Travis!" she screamed, and leaped over the railing and into the water. Rounds tore the railing apart where she'd been, sending pieces flying everywhere. She felt a something catch at her arm, and she splashed clumsily into the water.

She came to the surface about two meters from the tube, which should have been an easy swim. Except for the most excruciating pain and the fact that her right arm wasn't working. She almost fainted when she realized there was a foot-long splinter of wood piercing her upper arm.

She gritted her teeth and tried to swim toward the tube, just a simple sidestroke using her other arm. She was dimly aware of copious amounts of gunfire going on above her, but her focus was on her goal. Despite her efforts, the tube was receding from her.

How could that be? And then she realized that the tide was running out, carrying her away faster than she could swim.

Paladin, 03:48

Ophelia cursed. She'd launched a few more eyeballs as soon as she got back inside *Paladin*, but it had been too late to detect the enemy mercenaries. Now Travis was fighting two enemies with a damaged suit, and *Paladin* was vulnerable to enemy assault if they got past Travis—the hatch was still open. The sound of gunfire could be heard distinctly throughout the vehicle.

"*Uh, I could use some help here!*" Travis said, breathing heavily.

"*I'm coming up,*" Fang said.

Ophelia started to speak, but Armel cut her off. "Negative, Ghost One, I'ma take care of this."

She turned and looked at him, then realized he was accessing *Paladin's* fire controls. It wasn't his primary duty, but he could operate fire control from his console when he had to.

Jesus, firing at close range. She looked back at her drone view. It looked like Emily was in trouble, but still floating; more importantly, she was a safe distance from his likely blast zone. She moved an eyeball to give Armel a better view of the battlespace. Hidden from the view of the combatants, but not from her tiny drone, the APC's main gun elevated until it came out of the water underneath the walkway.

As the two mercenaries advanced on Travis' position, it fired once. A cyan bolt flashed and the screen went momentarily white. As the brightness dissipated and the scene gradually reappeared, ten feet of walkway around the blast was simply missing, as was the front of the building adjacent to the blast. The perimeter of the blast area was on fire. The two attacking mercenaries were nowhere to be seen.

"*Goddamit, I think you singed my eyebrows!*" Ghost Two bellowed.

Outside La Bomba, 03:55

Paiva followed the smoke, a highly visible beacon in infrared view, to the scene of the battle. Part of the walkway was still burning. The decrepit buildings had been so badly peppered by gunfire that they looked like they had the new chickenpox HX. Hawk Two was sprawled about five meters from the fire. He'd been bricked like Hawk Three had been earlier, but someone had uncoupled his helmet so he wouldn't suffocate inside the dead suit.

A bunch of dead Batista soldiers littered the walkway on the other side of the fire. Probably the rest of Squad One.

"Hey, boss," Raynald said. "The jamming stopped." Paiva translated that to mean that their opponents didn't think they needed jamming anymore and had probably retrieved the jammer for later use if necessary. "Got some eyeballs coming your way, too."

"Good," Paiva said. "The Monumentalists have managed to break contact."

"Shit, boss. And, uh, I'm not seein' vital—"

"Two is bricked. I think Four and Five are gone." It had been more than two years since he'd lost a fighter. Casualties were the worst part of this line of work, even though he knew it was an inevitable consequence of the mercenary trade.

"Oh, hell."

"I expect they're going to try to escape via the river. Let's see if we can head them off."

"On it."

Paiva hated failing at a mission.

He knew he had a crack team, and they'd traded blows with the Monumentalists like two heavyweight boxers in a world title match. And they'd lost.

At least for now.

24. EXFILTRATION

Paladin, 04:21

Emily came to gradually, becoming increasingly annoyed at the way *Khufu* was rolling in the waves of the Amazon River. After a while, she realized that there were people looking down at her and the ceiling above didn't look remotely like her cabin aboard the *Khufu*.

Well, let's see. That must mean she was aboard the *Paladin*. Those weren't waves; they were rolling along the uneven bottom. She was alive, so clearly she hadn't drowned. She could kind of feel her arm, but it seemed numb. She turned her head gradually. Yup, bandages.

"Where are we?" she croaked.

"Still in the *favela,*" Miller replied.

"They lookin' for us?"

"You bet your bottom dollar," Travis said.

"I know how to get out," she said tiredly. She closed her eyes for a minute, felt herself start to drift off. Forced them open again. Travis bent down over her and she whispered into his ear. She closed her eyes again. "We just…" Her voice faded out and her head lolled to one side as she passed out again.

Travis looked up at the concerned faces around Emily. "That's crazy," he said, then smiled. "It's so dumb, it might just work."

Paladin, 06:37

Dawn rose over a city shrouded in the smoke of the nighttime bombing. Some wooden buildings were still on fire and would continue burning until the late morning tropical rainfall quenched them.

Helicopters noisily criss-crossed the sky over the dark waters of the Rio Negro and the *favela* while armed soldiers filtered through the narrow walkways of the shantytown. They peered under walkways and buildings, used long poles or electronic devices to probe the canals, all searching for any traces of the mysterious quarry they'd been told to find.

With all official attention drawn to the beehive of activity of the river side of the *favela*, *Paladin* rolled ashore on the far side of the *favela*, sporting the drab olive color and markings of an official Batista military vehicle and pulling what looked like an eight-meter-long truck trailer in jungle camouflage colors.

Its exposure was about five seconds. If anybody associated with the Batistas had noticed a vehicle coming out of the water, well, that would have been noteworthy.

But after it was no longer in the water, after it had turned onto a road, it was just another official military vehicle, albeit a strange-looking one. And the further from the *favela* it got, the less noteworthy it was.

Inside *Paladin* an hour later, after Miller, their only Portuguese speaker, had helped them bullshit their way through a checkpoint to get out of the city, Travis looked at Fang and Ophelia, in turn. "I can't believe this worked."

Khufu, 09:45

Ester leaned over Kushner's bed and shook his shoulder. His eyes snapped open. "Any word?" he croaked.

"Nothing," Ester replied. They knew that all hell had broken loose last night, thanks to the Chinese bombing. And that a full-scale EMP had gone off. "But I've got something else to show you."

She pulled out a flexxi and folded it open so Kushner could see it. "I acquired a password to Ahoub's surveillance system." She smiled with a certain amount of satisfaction. "Looked over someone's shoulder while they were typing it."

"Old school," he said, "but effective."

She pressed a button on the screen. "This is January fourteenth, when you sent Emily to get tea." The screen showed her walking with the tray in her hands, on her way back to Kushner's cabin and the ongoing strategy session. But first, she stopped in front of her own cabin and went in. A moment later, she came out and continued on to Kushner's cabin.

"You may recall," Ester continued, "that when she came back, she made a point of personally fixing you a cup of tea."

Kushner clenched his teeth and looked up at her. "You're saying she infected me deliberately." His eyes were glittering with anger.

"Yes," she said. "I think so."

"That bitch! I'll destroy her." Kushner started coughing, painful hacking coughs that shook his frame. When they subsided, he said, "She'll never work in the art field again, never. I'll see to that."

War Zone, 10:19
Bang Hai, 238 km east of Manaus

"What do you mean, you can't find them?"

"Just that, sir. They've disappeared. The Batistas have forces all over the *favela* and the river looking for them."

"The Batistas? How are they involved?"

"There was some sort of running battle. We think the Monumentalists got the artwork, but were interrupted by a mercenary group called the Hawks. They work for a General Diego, of the Batistas, and were probably commissioned to transport the artwork to the buyer."

"So, the Monumentalists have the artwork? And we don't know where they are?"

"Yes, sir."

Favela, 11:41

Manuel was in his narrow bed, a grandiose name for what was really just a cot, napping through the heat of the mid-day, when he heard the scratching at his backdoor. Groaning, he sat up, ignoring the aches and pains as much as he could. Getting old was a burden, though it surely beat the alternatives.

He slipped his feet into some sandals. He remembered living in far finer places than this hovel in the *favela*, where one could actually walk on the floors without risking splinters. But that was before the Batistas and his fall from grace.

He shuffled his way slowly to the backdoor and opened it. A foreign woman was huddled in the doorway, blond and blue-eyed and surprisingly muscular. One side of her face was bruised, black and blue from her neck to her temple. She wore a hodgepodge of clothes, probably stolen, he noted, and she was dirt-covered and splattered with what looked like blood.

She was holding her side, clearly in pain, and breathing shallowly, as if breathing hurt. Maybe broken ribs, that would be consistent with what he was seeing.

"Are you…are you Manuel Barbosa?" she asked.

"I used to be," he said. "Now I'm just an old man living in the *favela*."

"Anton Ahoub…if there was trouble…I…" she said haltingly.

"Ah." The old man smiled. "Of course I'll help you." Ahoub had saved both of his granddaughters from slavers. A side effect of his fall from grace; his enemies had taken his family, too, except for the two girls that Ahoub had rescued. He bent down and, despite the pain in his back, lifted her up and helped her hobble into his meager home.

"I'm Laney," she said. "I should…warn you…" She sagged down onto his bed. "They're looking for me."

"The Batistas?"

"Yeah."

Manuel smiled. Even better. Two birds with one stone. Repay Ahoub and stick it to the Batistas. It was shaping up to be a lovely day.

Did You Enjoy This Book?

Please leave a review on Amazon, Goodreads, or your favorite online retailer.

Do You Want More?

Sign up for David Keener's monthly newsletter for news on future releases, plus get a free novelette, *The Jakarta Breach*, set in the same universe as this book:

www.davidkeener.org/newsletter

EXTRAS

Afterward

Find out how *Clash By Night* came to be created.

Bullets, Beer & Gear

The best, or at least most opinionated, newsletter for military professionals, police, mercenaries, beer drinkers, and gun lovers, brought to you monthly by Jo Jo's Ironmongery, the finest safety and surveillance (S&S) store in Los Angeles, California, and the entire Pacific Union.

Preview: Finders, Keepers

Cal McCallister is an ex-soldier and an ex-cop, living with his dog Fen and making ends meet as a private detective in a futuristic Los Angeles. His next case may be his last. Another thrilling SF crime story, set in the same world as *Clash by Night.*

AFTERWARD

In 2017, I was invited to participate in a rather unusual and intriguing anthology called *The Curator*. The premise was:

> When a salvage ship in the 26th century stumbles on the debris sphere of a long-lost colony transport, they're not expecting much. Spotting an intact cargo container within the debris, they're surprised. Especially when they discover it's still got power.
>
> Inside, a skeleton in a spacesuit, immediately dubbed "The Curator." And hundreds of lost, priceless paintings, all maintained at a safe temperature by an onboard fusion generator.

The idea was that each story in the anthology would be about a painting found in the cargo container, and the pictures of the paintings would be included in the volume. As a bonus, the origin of the mysterious "Curator" would be revealed through the stories and interstitial material.

For whatever reason, the semi-curated pool of writers tapped for the anthology didn't produce enough stories. And nobody wanted to open it to the wide world because…well, the word "deluge" comes to mind. Meanwhile, my own anthology contribution was going badly, nay, disastrously.

I had envisioned a short story that took place during the escape after a heist had already been completed. However, enough heist details were provided to pique the interest of readers. The members of my writing group were almost unanimous in wanting to read more about the heist.

So I added some chapters before the escape. But then, I had too much action, and there was no setup to establish the diverse crew of characters in the minds of readers. So I added more chapters before the chapters I'd just written.

Whew, what a mess.

I let the story stew for a month, reread it with a bit of distance and decided that it had evolved into a full-scale heist story.

A very unsatisfying one, because it didn't adhere even remotely to any of the tropes expected of a heist story.

I added even *more* chapters to the front of the story, and also corrected the trope-related issues. If you're thinking there's possibly a trend here, yup, you're right. I literally wrote the story backward (this is *not* a recommended writing technique).

Through it all, I never stopped believing in the story. I just kept plugging away at it until I finally ended up with what I felt was a fun, satisfying mashup: a heist story *and* a military SF story.

As you might expect, with all of the oft-repeated addition of chapters, the story just kept growing. I quipped to my writing group that it had turned into the "Story that Ate Cleveland."

I expected it to be too long for the anthology, but it turned out that my story was the perfect length to bring the anthology up to the expected word count.

Despite the hurdles in the writing process, I feel I ultimately ended up with a fun mashup. I hope you've enjoyed reading *Clash By Night* as much as I enjoyed… ahem…finishing it.

David Keener
March 22, 2021
Ashburn, Virginia

P.S. – I liked the end result so much that I'm already planning more stories with Emily, Ghost Team, and, maybe, just maybe, those pesky Hawks.

BULLETS, BEER & GEAR

AN OPINIONATED NEWSLETTER FROM JO JO'S IRONMONGERY

ISSUE 204 : APRIL 2114

One thing we've come to realize here at Jo Jo's Ironmongery...our customers LOVE their TRI-D shows. We know this because they come into our store and they ask to buy the gear they've seen in the latest flicks like *The Jakarta Connection*, *Living by the Gun*, *Mercenary*, and the new Mathilde Bond outing, *Killshot*, starring the incomparable Adeline Parkes.

In this edition of our illustrious newsletter, we're going to set the record straight. Here, for your benefit, is a compendium of interesting gear featured in these shows. Some of the gear doesn't actually exist. Of the gear that does exist, sadly, not all of it's gonna be stuff we're legally allowed to sell.

Enjoy. And remember, we're your one-stop shop for all your weaponry and surveillance needs.

BULLETS

Bedtime Special: Nickname for BT-102 ammo from Bayes-Truman, under exclusive contract to the United States military forces. Upon hitting a target wearing combat armor, the round releases a massive electrical surge that incapacitates the poor sucker within and also fries the circuitry in the combat suit. Military personnel refer to the effect as being "bricked."

Price: $$$
Notes: We can sell it if we can get it, but it's hard to get, unless you're making a TRI-D flick (in which case the suppliers seem to pop up out of the damn woodwork). While a Bedtime Special is technically non-lethal, some zappees have died from combat suit life support failures. Translation: if you get hit, you best hope one of your buddies remembers to crack open your damn helmet. And, yes, we've seen demos…it absolutely looks just as bad-ass as it did in *Killshot.*
Notes 2: Also available in a grenade version, nicknamed a "Buzz" grenade.

SOS Ammunition: All right boyos, we've got the perfect ammo for all you hunters, especially for those times when the deer are fightin' back…it's the SOS (Selectable, Optimized, Smart) brand from Weston Labs. Expensive as hell, but hey, if you know where the deer is, you don't even need a rifle. You can kill it with a pistol like the Heckler-Koch SP47x Smart Pistol.

Each round is a tiny rocket with significant down-range maneuverability and selectable effects: Normal, Penetrating, Incendiary, Explosive, and Optimal. Yes, with Optimal this baby can even use a directed explosion to deflect around corners (and trees).

Let's just say that a deer hidin' behind a tree ain't gonna be an option with these babies. 'Course, don't be using the Incendiary or Explosive options if'n your goal is venison.

Price: $$
Notes: We sell a lot of this ammo to mercenary units and security professionals. Licenses required.

BEER

We got two beers for you in this issue, one you can drink with your Significant Other, and one you can drink with your douche bag buddies. Pop Quiz: You get to figure out which one is which.

Indonesian Pale Ale: A very nice local beer from Stark Craft Beer, brewed in the north of Bali with pure spring water from Batu Karu Mountain (we got this from their site). Featured prominently in *The Jakarta Connection*.

EMP: The notorious Enhanced Mead Product (EMP) kicks like a mule with anger management issues. Nothing makes a day of critter-whomping better than being drunk off your ass (but please remember to shoot responsibly). It's so high-proof, it's illegal in some jurisdictions.

GEAR

boost: Slang for any pharmaceutical that enhances, or boosts, a person's innate capabilities in some way.

Common enhancements include: alertness/clarity, concentration, intelligence, speed, strength, etc. Some boosts have undesirable side effects, especially with black market versions. Most incur some sort of delayed cost, such as a period of downtime after usage.

> *Price:* $$
> *Notes:* We're serious 'bout the downtime. As they say on the street, "You boost, then you roost." While we don't deal in boosts, we do offer referrals and introductions to reputable producers for our Platinum members.

Chameleon suit: A top-of-the-line military combat suit for elite units. Has every feature of a top combat suit, plus a chameleon capability that renders the suit invisible to the standard visual spectrum and infrared. For infrared obscurement, heat can only be contained for a limited time before venting is required.

> *Price:* Doesn't matter.
> *Notes:* Mil-spec only. Even in the Republic of Texas, you need military connections to get these babies. But they are saaaaweeeeeeeeeeeeeettttt.

combat suit: Sophisticated body armor for the experienced combat specialist, with sensorium connectivity for integrated real-time status reporting, health optimization and combat operation. We carry all the major brands, including CrystalFLEX, HeavyD, RayBond XG and more. Typical brand-specific options include AI-support, skill modules, combat enhancing pharmaceuticals (illegal in most jurisdictions without proper licensing), replaceable armor panels, ablative coatings, power assist, and many more.

> *Price:* $ - $$$$
> *Notes:* If you need it, we got it. And in a range of colors, from the ever-popular black to bubblegum pink. Totally not joking. Yes, we had a rock band order a pink combat suit once.

Eyeball: A globular drone, six centimeters (that's 4.2 inches for all of you Luddites) in diameter, filled with sophisticated electronics and sensors. Propelled by multiple air jets. Numerous brands are available.

> *Price:* $ - $$$
> *Notes:* If you can afford them, we import mil-class hardened eyeballs from the Republic of Texas.
> *Notes 2:* If you don't know what a Luddite is, look it up on the Interweb-thingy, that's what it's for.

flybaby: A generic term for a small, disposable communication micro-drone, with different models available from diverse suppliers. Typically, solar-powered. Size ranges from about half a centimeter in diameter to barely visible. Flybabies float easily and quietly on a tiny air jet. Can be hard to detect when operating in passive sensory mode. Their small size is not consistent with the hardening necessary for survival in modern battle (for all y'all reading-challenged folks out there, that means they're as fragile as a good afterglow with a talkative partner), so they are often used in general support roles. Typically deployed in swarms.

Price: $ - $$
Notes: We got all types and all kinds, no matter what your surveillance needs are.

Heckler-Koch SP47x Smart Pistol: A rugged, reliable and impeccably engineered weapon that's perfect for just about any situation you'll ever find outside of a war zone. Integrates well with combat suits and sensoriums. Performance can also be dramatically augmented by numerous brands of smart ammunition, include our specially featured SOS ammo from Weston Labs. Featured in *Living by the Gun.*

Price: $$
Notes: With its high performance and reasonable cost, this pistol is one of our absolute best-selling weapons. Perfect for home defense and varmint control (both the four-legged and two-legged varieties).

Hunter/killer (H/K): An automated drone that detects, tracks and destroys other drones. Often released as a horde to establish sensory control of a local battlespace.

Price: Doesn't matter.
Notes: Sorry, buckoes, but we ain't sellin' these. Do you have ANY idea how much trouble we'd be in if'n one of

you yahoos used our H/K's for a bank robbery or something? Try Texas, those folks will sell anything.

jammer: A generic term for a drone that blocks radio communication frequencies in an area. Available in many models from diverse suppliers. Size, level of hardening, general survivability and range of effect vary widely based on the model.

Price: $$$
Notes: If you're not from a licensed merc unit, you can't buy one…try Texas. Also, please stop asking us about the convenient pen version that was featured in *Killshot.* As far as we know, ain't nobody that makes that.

Marauder Pistol: This pistol from Horton Ltd. in Australia is optimized for combat suits with power assist. It is large, rugged, reliable, and kicks like a boosted elephant. It's the go-to sidearm for more merc units than you can shake a stick at.

Price: $$$
Notes: We sell a lot of these, primarily to professionals in security firms, mercenary outfits and SWAT units. Used in *Mercenary* by the Black Adders merc unit.

Minelayer: A man-portable weapon that deploys powerful, pellet-sized landmines sprayed in a selectable pattern. The mines are easily programmable for the ultimate in area deterrence. There are models available from several different vendors. Minelayers usually include

20 to 100 pellets per factory-sealed magazine.

> *Price:* Nope.
> *Notes:* Military or merc unit use only. The ones you saw in *Killshot* were used very effectively.

mini-EMP: A high-tech, non-nuclear device for generating an Electro-Magnetic Pulse (EMP) within a limited area. Mini-EMP devices are available in a range of sizes, as defined by their area of effect, ranging from several city blocks to several square kilometers.

> *Price:* What the HELL are you thinkin'?
> *Notes:* Just 'cause one of these babies was featured in *Killshot*, we don't sell these. They're highly illegal—restricted to military forces and serious merc units.

pulse gun: A generic class of non-lethal, short-range weapons that disable a target with pulsed microwaves. Available in a variety of sizes and options from multiple vendors.

> *Price:* $
> *Notes:* We sell a lot of these for both home and personal defense. Some models can easily fit in a jacket pocket or purse. We also sell a bunch to security services that need non-lethal stopping power.

Samson X4 Rifle Launcher: Smart Mexican rifle that fires brilliant explosive rounds with limited onboard propulsion for in-flight targeting optimization. Can fire coordinated bursts of three rounds. Features simple integration with combat suits and sensoriums for the ultimate in "see it, kill it" effectiveness.

> *Price:* $$$
> *Notes:* No 'bout a doubt it. This is a hot weapon. It's one of our best-sellers and we have a variety of types of ammo for it. You'll need appropriate licenses at the pol, mil or merc level to purchase some types of ammo, especially the explosive varieties.
> *Notes 2:* No, it doesn't launch rifles (though that's a bizarre image). The next person that asks that question will lose their range privileges for a year.

sensorium: An integrated suite of electro/nano enhancements to the human brain. Typical augmenttations include vision overlays, GPS, maps, integrated comms, memory enhancements and automated information searches. More advanced augmentations include behavior mods, reflex overlays, automated threat assessment, skill downloads and more.

Sensorium modifications are typically done in childhood, for best adaptation by recipients. Only available in more advanced countries and generally for middle-class or higher income levels.

Numerous augmentations are available legally. Additionally, many augmentations of varying and questionable merit are available on the black market.

Price: $ - $$$$
Notes: Folks, this ain't our specialty. For augmentations, we recommend Dr Shock's Emporium. Despite the TRI-D hype (man, those commercials are *awesome*), they're the best at what they do in all of Los Angeles, and maybe even the entire Pacific Union.

Skill module: Also known as a "skip," as in you get a skill while skipping all that boring learning time. A sensorium enhancement (or elite combat suit enhancement) that provides a user with an additional skill or set of skills that they did not previously possess. There are even rumors that some skips have a limited ability to initiate bodily actions, like attack evasion, without prior volition on the part of the user. Very controversial and largely unregulated.

Price: N/A
Notes: Look, we don't sell these. They're illegal, experimental, and dangerous. The only skips we know of that get serious safety testing are mil-spec skips for use in high-end military gear.
Notes 2: Yes, the black market Zeus combat mod shown in *Living by the Gun* is real. But we don't have it. We don't sell it. And we got no idea where to get it. Nobody even knows who makes it. But we have seen a demo, and it is *serious mojo.*

PREVIEW

Turn the page for an excerpt from *Finders, Keepers*, the next thrilling novel from David Keener, set in Los Angeles in the same futuristic world as *Clash by Night.*

In a world where clones are the new slave class, private detective Cal McCallister has just been paid a lot of cash to find an unregistered clone named Claudia who's been snatched by a black market team of clone hunters. He'll need all of his skills as an ex-soldier and an ex-cop to bring Claudia home. One thing for sure, he's going to need the help of his dog Fen.

Also featuring Gavin McCloud, the younger brother of Travis McCloud, from *Clash by Night.*

FINDERS, KEEPERS

Preview

I. The Case (or, Why Does It Always Start with a Dame?)

Mowbray Lounge, in Little Texas: Sunday, 17:00, 2114 — Missing 16 Hours

The Mowbray Lounge (called the M), more than seedy but less than sleazy, was a restaurant and an entertainment venue with a stage for comedians, dancers, karaoke, you name it. The two things that rescued it from obscurity were the best BBQ and ribs in Little Texas, and the thrice-weekly Dance Nights, where professionals and wannabes strutted their stuff.

The blond woman looked totally out of place sitting alone in one of the back booths, wearing a designer business suit with creases sharp enough to draw blood. She was obviously uninterested in the racy dance routine being enacted on the stage, which I cleverly deduced by the fact that she had her back to the action.

I figured the woman was either my client or somebody had picked a bad place to go slumming.

As I approached, a man sidled up to her table. I'd have recognized that cocky shuffle anywhere, even if his name, alias, and priors hadn't popped up on the edge of my sensorium.

Jaeger, real name Bartholomew Jones.

He'd been out of circulation for a while. He should have stayed there.

Jaeger was dressed street lethal, but flashier than I remembered. He had Snake gang tats entwining his arms, a fluorescent red Mohawk and a crooked nose that looked like it had been broken a few times. He was way out of his territory; the Snakes mostly dominated East L.A. above the 60. He said something to the woman. She obviously didn't like it, because she dashed the drink she'd been nursing into his face.

While he was distracted, I took three fast strides, cupped his head, and slammed it into the table. Hard, like I was dunking a basketball.

And then I did it again, just for good measure.

I shoved him aside. He sprawled on the floor, looked up at me blearily, but still had the presence of mind to extend razor-sharp fighting claws from his fingers.

"Gonna cut you up for that," he threatened.

"Go ahead, tosser, if you wanna lose those claws again."

When I'd still been a cop, Jaeger had used his previous set of claws on one of my snitches and left her face so badly scarred it had taken a couple of years before I could put together a deal with enough of a windfall to get her fixed. Now she was married with two kids and nobody except her husband and me knew she'd ever been a Tinsel Town streetwalker.

Street rules had dictated that I take Jaeger down hard for that. I'd thrashed him within an inch of his life, and then smashed his fingers and claws into splinters with a sledgehammer.

I was disappointed to see he'd apparently done well for himself in the intervening years. Well enough to get all my fine handiwork repaired.

He sneered at me. "You ain't a cop no more."

"You should be afraid," I said, smiling. "Now I don't have to follow any rules." For some reason, nobody except my dog finds my smiles comforting.

Jaeger scuttled backwards without taking his eyes off me. I had cyber mods from my stint in the military; he knew how fast I could move if I needed to.

As it turned out, I didn't have to worry about Jaeger. The bouncer loomed behind him, then reached down and tapped him with a military-grade taser. There was a bright arc accompanied by a snapping sizzle, then Jaeger arched his back in agony before going limp. Out stone cold.

And me without my sledgehammer.

"Thanks, Gavin," I said.

"Don't be startin' stuff in here," Gavin McCloud said mildly. "You'll waste away to a shadow if I have to drop a three-week ban on you, like this loco hombre's gonna get." Gavin was ex-military like me, though he was Republic of Texas and I was U.S.A. His mods were probably better than mine—the U.S.A. was much diminished, in both size and manufacturing prowess, after the Time of Troubles and the Second Civil War.

"Didn't start it," I said. "He was bothering my client here." I turned to the woman. "You're Ester Waynewright?"

"Yes." I noticed she was holding a pulse gun in her lap, a small, easy to conceal gun that quietly fired disabling microwave pulses. Not so helpless, after all. "He asked me if I liked pole dancing. Said he had a pole to show me."

I shot a glance at Gavin. "Eight-week ban…for unoriginality?"

He shook his head sadly. "They just don't make thugs like they used to. Yeah, I think you're right." He looked down at Ester. "Sorry about the trouble, ma'am. The drink is on the house, and I'll get you another one for free."

"No thanks."

Gavin smiled easily. "Rain check, then."

I sat down across from Ester as Gavin effortlessly hoisted Jaeger over his shoulder and carried him away.

"It was actually a very nice Vodka Collins," she said regretfully. "I wasted a perfectly good drink on that idiot."

"So, what brings you to need my services?"

She looked around. "Is there somewhere more private where we can talk?"

"Sure. My office is just around the corner."

A few minutes later we were traipsing around the aforementioned corner. I gestured to a squat, rugged-looking vehicle that looked like the illicit love child of an RV and a U.S. Army troop carrier. Which was a surprisingly apt description; there'd been a lot of surplus gear lying around after the Second War Between the States. It was as long as a bus, but low-slung and slightly wider. It looked like it had seen better days. It had a California license plate that read "GRENDEL" and a bumper sticker right above it that said, "DOG is my Co-Pilot."

Ester shot me a look. "That's your office?"

"Convenient, eh? I can park it anywhere."

I ran my hand over the door access sensor. There was a click as the locks released.

I turned and saw Ester looking at the "BEWARE OF DOG" sticker I'd put right above the sensor.

"I'm guessing you have a dog?"

"You're about to meet him," I said, pushing the door open. "Don't worry, he hasn't eaten anybody in over a week."

"Really?"

"Yeah, I've got him on a diet."

Her eyes widened as my dog suddenly filled the doorway, tail wagging like a propeller. Two hundred and twenty pounds of gengineered canine, part wolf with some Rottweiler and mastiff tossed in for good measure.

He had a huge head, an improbably wide chest, legs like furry pillars and scarred ears. Elevated by the two steps that it took to climb into the vehicle, he was basically at eye level for Ester.

"You don't have many problems with people breaking into your office, do you?"

"Not lately," I said. "That was actually the last person he ate. This is Fen, by the way."

She chuckled and held out her hand for Fen to sniff. "Short for Fenrir, right?"

"I guess you know your Norse mythology." I was impressed. Most people didn't pick up the reference to the Norse wolf god. It was a much more suitable name than the nickname he'd had before I got him.

Smiling, Ester brushed away a lock of hair that had fallen across her eyes. "I always liked mythology in general, not just Norse mythology. It made me wonder, though. If that's what people believed in the past, what are they going to believe in the future?"

Fen let her rub his ears and stroke his head, which was even more impressive. He was friendly, but he didn't take to everybody.

"I always wanted a dog," she said wistfully.

"So get a dog."

"Maybe someday." She sounded like she didn't expect that day to ever come, which seemed odd. Judging by her expensive outfit, casual assurance and personal weaponry, she seemed like someone who had both money and connections. Certainly not somebody to be stymied in having a pet if that was what she really wanted.

"Out of the way, you big lug," I said, pushing Fen aside so we could enter.

Inside, you couldn't really tell that the RV was actually a converted troop carrier unless you knew what to look for. Like the low ceiling or the thinly disguised armored doors leading, respectively, to the back compartment of the vehicle and the cockpit.

Otherwise, it had the normal accoutrements of an RV, including a mini-kitchen, a fold-down table with bench seating that I used for a desk and a couch facing a wall-mounted Tri-D projector. The back compartment included a modest-sized bedroom, guest accommodations (bunk beds), the privy, and a secure compartment I used as an armory.

What I really had was a bullet-proof RV with a killer commo suite and the world's worst suspension. And I mean worst. Sometimes I swear it generated bumps if the road was too smooth.

A client hadn't had the cash to pay for a job that had been more complicated and dangerous than expected. We'd agreed that *Grendel*—that's what I'd named my vehicle—was adequate compensation for the job. I'd been living in it ever since.

I gestured for Ester to take a seat at the kitchen table. While Fen circled three times and then lay down on her foot, I sat opposite her and raised an eyebrow.

"We lost an employee," Ester said. "We need you to get her back."

"Who's we?"

"You don't need to know."

"Name?"

"Claudia Vazquez."

"What's she do?"

"You don't need to know that, either."

I sighed. Sometimes you get clients who think they know best what you need to know. They're usually wrong. "I work better when I have all the necessary information."

"Indeed," she said, smiling. "But you still don't need to know that."

"All right. How do you know she's lost?"

"She's tapped. We have footage that shows her being grabbed by some thugs." She held up a memnode, a shiny device about the size of a fingernail.

I raised an eyebrow. A tap rig meant whoever had the right access codes could see, hear and record everything that the tapped individual experienced. Most people preferred their privacy.

I took the memnode from her. "When was she taken?"

"Last night. Little after midnight."

"So, she's been missing for around sixteen hours," I said. "It's probably going to complicate things." That was an understatement. With any abduction, time is your enemy. Depending on what the kidnappers wanted, she could already have been raped, chopped up for body parts or moved to some remote location. They should have contacted me, or the police, as soon as possible.

"I know," Ester said. "It took too long to convince my employer."

"I have to be honest, most kidnapping cases are solved in forty-eight hours…or they're not solved at all."

"I know the stats."

Flipping open a panel on the wall just above the table, I inserted the device into a slot. Glancing down and to the right, the file list popped into view in my sensorium. There were two files on the memnode, a large video file and a small one. I picked the smaller one, which began playing on the wall above the panel.

POV of someone sitting in a crowded night club with loud, techno-cowboy music. Whoever it was reached for a drink on the bar. A woman, judging by the non-masculine arm, the bejeweled bangles and the cherry-red nail polish. The club's clientele was a mix of men and women, maybe a little on the rough side. I was pretty sure I wasn't looking at a genteel, up-scale establishment.

At my inquiring glance, Ester said, "The Mixie Trixie." I'd heard of it. A pickup club on the edge of Thai Town.

Claudia exchanged some unintelligible words with another woman at the bar. Enhancement would bring out the words later, if they mattered. She got up and walked toward the back of the club, obviously heading for the facilities. After taking care of business, during which Ester and I both studiously looked away from the view, Claudia adjusted her make-up in front of the mirror. There were some good close-ups of her face, so I'd have a good image to show around. A few minutes later, someone hit her with a taser as she came out of the ladies' room.

The view swung wildly as her attackers, and there were at least two of them, carried her down the hallway and though a door into a back alley. The footage never showed a clear view of the attackers, though there was one good silhouette of a man's head outlined in the glare from the light above the back door. He had spiky hair and big ears with holes in the lobes.

The view went away when someone pulled a Faraday bag over Claudia's head.

I looked over at Ester. The corners of her eyes were shiny with unshed tears. "I'll need to see all of the footage of her at the club."

"It's on there," she said. "That was just a clip of the actual abduction."

"She was clearly targeted," I said. "That wasn't a random kidnapping. So, there's something you're not telling me."

"She's a clone."

I raised an eyebrow. Legally, clones weren't people, except in the Republic of Texas.

They'd come into heavy usage before Civil War II, during the world-wide Time of Troubles. It had been a mad, world-wide paroxysm of war that had stopped just short of apocalypse, not that that mattered to the billions that died from conflicts, tactical nukes, man-made plagues, digital assassinations and the like. Fast-grown clones with rough-shod cerebral programming had been used for dangerous jobs like cleaning up plague victims, medical experimentation, cannon fodder…you name it.

Now, clones were too useful for spare body parts, cheap labor, whatever folks needed and didn't want to do themselves. The new slave class. Just like you and me, but not, because of various genetic markers added during the cloning process.

"Is that a problem for you?" Ester asked.

"Not if you pay me enough," I said.

"We can do that."

I leaned back. Whatever her role was with her employer, negotiation clearly wasn't part of her job description. "It just means we're going to be dealing with a rough crowd."

"Is that all it takes for you? Money." She sounded disappointed.

"Money always helps, sweetheart," I said. "It's the universal lubricant. But, no, the way I figure it, anything that can have a meaningful conversation with me is a person. And I don't believe in slavery."

ABOUT THE AUTHOR

David Keener is an author, editor and public speaker who lives in Northern Virginia with his wife and two (oops, three) inordinately large dogs. He writes SF, Fantasy and Mystery but loves the idea of mashing up his favorite genres in new and unexpected ways.

He is the grand instigator behind the *Worlds Enough* anthology series, and co-editor of the first two volumes, *Fantastic Defenders and Fantastic Detectives*. His next anthology will be *The Forever Inn*, about a mysterious inn that travels randomly throughout the multiverse.

He is a founding member of the *Hourlings Podcast Project*, covering writing-related topics. He frequently speaks at conventions, where he often conducts writing workshops. Find out more about him at:

Newsletter: http://www.davidkeener.org/newsletter
Website: http://www.davidkeener.org
FaceBook: DavidKeenerWrites

ACKNOWLEDGMENTS

As usual, a whole bunch of people helped me with this story, including: Don Anderson, Evan Friedman, Elizabeth Hayes, Steve Keener, Amanda Kryway, Donna Royston and Martin Wilsey. And many thanks to my writing group, the Hourlings.

Thanks are due famed mystery writer Lawrence Block, whose anthology, *In Sunlight or In Shadow: Stories Inspired by the Paintings of Edward Hopper*, provided the thematic inspiration for incorporating actual artwork into this story.

Kudos to the Metropolitan Museum of Art for releasing rights-free digital copies of much of their vast art collection to the public. Now you know where these beautiful art pieces came from.

Also, a special acknowledgment to Henry Kuttner, who published his classic novella "Clash by Night" in 1943, set on the dangerous seas of the semi-feudal world of Venus. It's been 78 years; I don't think he'd begrudge me reusing the title.

Finally, I would be remiss if I did not mention the influence of *The Monuments Men* on this story. First with the 2014 film, and subsequently the excellent non-fiction account the film was based on, by Robert M. Edsel with Brad Witter.

Leading a busy life? Check out these Quick Reads!

The Rooftop Game: Lydio Malik is the Royal Bodyguard for the infant Princess Analisa. He'll do anything to protect his charge. When the king's enemies breach the castle, he takes refuge on the roof of the highest tower. If they want her…they're going to pay the cost in blood.

The Whispering Voice: Anna Brodie has two hours to rob a bank, or thugs will kill her family. What the bad guys don't know is…she has supernatural help.

An Unlikely Hero: Malcolm Jameson has lost everything and is about to end his life by leaping from a bridge. Then a passing bicyclist hands him a Magic Book. And his life will never be the same again.

What are *you* waiting for? Adventure awaits!

IMAGE CREDITS

Metropolitan Museum of Art, Public Domain (CC0)

- **The Chess Players:** by Thomas Eakins, 1876.
- **The Dancers:** by Edgar Degas, around 1900.
- **The Gulf Stream:** by Winslow Homer, 1899.
- **The Harvesters:** by Pieter Bruegel the Elder, 1565.
- **Madame Theodore Gobillard:** by Edgar Degas, 1869.
- **The Veteran in a New Field:** by Winslow Homer, 1865.
- **Wheat Field With Cypresses:** by Vincent Van Gogh, 1889.

Other Images & Fonts

- **Amazon Map:** Copyright © 2021 by David Keener. All rights reserved.
- **Carnivalee Freakshow:** A font from Christopher Hansen, free for commercial and personal use.
- **David Keener in Paris:** Copyright © 2021 by David Keener. All rights reserved.
- **Fyodor Bold:** A font from Blue Room Collective, free for commercial and personal use.
- **H.H. Agallas:** A font from deFharo, free for commercial and personal use.
- **Title/Author:** Copyright © 2021 by David Keener. All rights reserved.

www.ingramcontent.com/pod-product-compliance
Lightning Source LLC
Chambersburg PA
CBHW020558310726
48979CB00008B/1260/J
* 9 7 8 1 9 4 5 9 9 4 7 8 4 *